THE GREEK'S
BLACKMAILED
MISTRESS

THE GREEK'S BLACKMAILED MISTRESS

LYNNE GRAHAM

MILLS & BOON

First published in Great Britain 2018
by Mills & Boon, an imprint of HarperCollins*Publishers*
1 London Bridge Street, London, SE1 9GF

Large Print edition 2019

© 2018 Lynne Graham

ISBN: 978-0-263-07883-1

MIX
Paper from
responsible sources
FSC® C007454

This book is produced from independently certified
FSC™ paper to ensure responsible forest management.
For more information visit www.harpercollins.co.uk/green.

Printed and bound in Great Britain
by CPI Group (UK) Ltd, Croydon, CR0 4YY

CHAPTER ONE

'I'M TOO BEAUTIFUL to be dumped,' Fabiana told Xan in all seriousness, her perfect face a mask of disbelief. 'It's my poor English, isn't it? I'm picking you up wrong—'

'No,' Xan contradicted with gravity, smoothly switching to her native Spanish. 'The movers will be here in an hour to help you pack. We've been together two months. I did tell you that this arrangement wouldn't last any longer than that—'

'But you can't *not* want me any more—' Giving her reflection an appreciative appraisal in the nearest mirror, Fabiana fluffed up her fall of tumbling dark curls.

'I *don't* want you any more,' Xan countered, losing patience, beginning to wonder how the hell he had enjoyed even one encounter with the brunette, infused as she was with astronomical vanity.

'Where am I supposed to go?' Fabiana demanded abruptly, studying him in frustration, silently recognising that she was unlikely to ever have a better-looking man in her bed. Six foot three and beautifully built, his black hair cropped short over a lean, devastatingly handsome face, the Greek financial guru, Xan Ziakis, would be a very hard act to follow and without him she would lose access to the exclusive events she had so much enjoyed.

'Your possessions will be stored and a hotel room has been engaged for you,' Xan clarified, on firmer ground now because he had been changing mistresses every couple of months for years. There was nothing new about the status quo and Fabiana had benefitted richly from their association even though his visits had been few.

Reflecting on that last surprising truth, Xan questioned his libido. He was only thirty years old. Obviously he was bored with Fabiana, he told himself impatiently. Yet, in truth, work and the pursuit of profit had always won out over the thrill of sex for Xan. *Some day* he would heed his mother's endless pleas and start dating with a view to taking a wife but that day was many years off. His father, Helios, had married five times over, gifting Xan with a costly and troublesome flock of half-siblings, and he was determined not to repeat his father's mistakes. Helios had married too young while Xan intended to wait until he was in his forties, at the very least, and had sown every last wild oat available to him.

Not that Fabiana and her faceless, virtually indistinguishable predecessors had much in common with wild oats, he conceded with wry self-mockery. All his bed partners had been models or minor actresses, the sort of women who understood that he paid generously for everything they wanted in return for their bodies. Framed in those words, it sounded crude, he acknowledged without shame, but that very basic format worked well for him and the one time he had tried another approach, when he had been both young and idealistic, it had gone badly wrong for him.

Xan believed love was a dangerous risk. His father had fallen in love repeatedly with demonstrably unsuitable women. Xan had had his heart broken when he was only twenty-one and nothing would've persuaded him to revisit that learning experience.

A financial genius, who had become a billionaire by the age of twenty-five, Xan was the acclaimed mastermind behind City coups worth billions. He had quickly repaired the giant hole in the Ziakis family fortunes left by his imprudent father, and had simply chosen to organise his sex life much as he organised everything else around him because disorder of any kind put him in a bad mood. He liked his life smooth; he *preferred* a routine he virtually never deviated from. He would not risk the upheaval of marriage breakdowns and hugely expensive divorces that had decimated his father's wealth. He was stronger than that and infinitely cleverer, indeed smarter than most of the people around him, and the only risks he took were in the financial field where he trusted his gut and aggressive instincts.

His phone vibrated, instantly freeing him from all awareness of Fabiana's presence. He dug it out, immediately wondering why Dmitri, the head of his security team, would be contacting him. A moment later, he found out and he was enraged. Someone had *dared* to steal something very precious from him, and he stalked out of the apartment his mistresses used without another word to the brunette. His penthouse apartment was his sanctuary where he entertained neither women nor anyone else. The idea that *any* person could violate his London home in spite of all the security he had put in place sent his hot temper nuclear.

'*The maid?*' he breathed with audible distaste.

'Or her son. She let him into the apartment

even though it's against the rules,' Dmitri filled in stiffly. 'I could pursue this discreetly *or* call the police—'

'You call the police and provide them with the evidence,' Xan cut in fiercely. 'You punish them with the full weight of the law!'

Xan collected imperial jade that cost him shocking sums and he had placed that little brush pot in the hall for his own enjoyment because it was a remarkably tactile piece and had once belonged to a Chinese emperor. In his penal frame of mind, whipping was too light a punishment for thieves.

The following day, Elvi's teenaged brother flung himself into her arms and sobbed, 'I'm so sorry…this whole nightmare is *my* fault!'

'Let's calm down,' Elvi suggested gently, framing her little brother's face with both small hands, recognising from the anguish in his green eyes that he had been crying alone in his room for some time. 'I'll make some tea—'

'I don't want tea!' Daniel protested. 'I want to go down to the police station and admit it was me and *not* Mum!'

'No, we're going to talk about this first,' Elvi overruled. 'Mum protected you for a reason—'

'Bloody medical school! It doesn't matter—'

Of course it mattered, Elvi thought ruefully, that Daniel wanted to be a doctor like their late father. It was all he had ever wanted to be since he was a little boy and a conviction for theft would totally destroy that ambition. Furthermore, Daniel had already been awarded a place at Oxford to study because his academic results were the very best. She knew exactly why her mother had lied and taken the blame for her son, but what she could not understand or credit was that Daniel would *ever* have stolen anything.

'I *need* to know what happened,' she persisted quietly, seating herself on the bed where her dark-haired brother had flopped down to hang his head. He was getting so tall and lanky at just past eighteen that he was fast growing out of all his clothes, his jeans barely reaching his ankles and his enormous feet. She and Daniel bore not an ounce of resemblance to each other because, although they had had the same father, they had had different mothers. Elvi's mother had died when she was a baby, and her father's second wife had adopted her and brought her up as her own. She was the short, plump one of the family, Elvi conceded ruefully, bright blue eyes troubled, pushing back the white-blonde hair sticking to her perspiring brow because she had run all the way home from work as soon as Daniel had phoned her.

'Yesterday, I called to pick up Mum for her AA meeting but I was a bit early,' Daniel confided.

Elvi heaved a sigh, for both of them tried to ensure that their mother went to regular meetings and since the summer arrived and Daniel had finished school and only contrived to find part-time employment, he had taken over the duty. Sally Cartwright deserved her family's support to stay sober. She had been sober now for three long wonderful years but Elvi was painfully aware that alcoholism was an affliction that never entirely went away. Denying herself the craving for that one dangerous drink was what Sally dealt with every day.

'*And?*'

'She was cleaning something and had to finish it, so she told me to sit down in the hall and not to touch anything,' Daniel grumbled. 'Like I was a little kid or something and I was annoyed, so I *didn't* listen...'

'What did you touch?' Elvi almost whispered.

'There was this little jade pot sitting on the console table in a patch of sunlight—honestly, Elvi...it was the sort of thing I've only ever seen inside a museum case—and I just wanted to hold it for a minute, so I picked it up and took it over to the window to hold it up to the light because it was so delicate—'

'And then what?' Elvi prompted with anxious impatience.

Daniel studied her in almost childlike discomfiture. 'Then the doorbell went and Mum rushed out to answer it and I kept the pot hidden in my hand because I didn't want her to see what I'd been doing. Unluckily for me, the man at the door worked for Mr Ziakis too and he was there to tell me that I shouldn't be in the apartment in the first place and that I should be waiting for my mother downstairs. He made me leave immediately, like…he was sort of nice about it but I had no chance of putting the pot back with him standing there—'

'For goodness' sake, Daniel!' Elvi erupted in vehement protest. 'You should've handed it to him straight away! The minute you stepped out of that apartment door with it, you labelled yourself a thief—'

'Yeah, you think I don't know that now?' Daniel traded with laden irony. 'But I gave way to panic and I concealed it, brought it home and stuck the blasted thing in a drawer. I planned to ask Mum to put it back for me tomorrow but apparently the housekeeper reported it missing when she turned in for work in the evening, so that was that. I missed the boat and—'

Stupid, stupid, stupid, repeated in Elvi's head but she didn't let the word pass her lips because she could see that her sibling was already painfully aware that he had acted like an impulsive and reckless total idiot. 'When did the police get involved?' she interposed.

'This morning…they arrived with a search warrant and of course they found it. Mum asked me to go into her room to get her handbag and while I was in there she may have confessed to taking it because by the time I came back out again because I couldn't find the blasted thing she was being arrested and read her rights,' he revealed chokily, gulping back more unmanly sobs. 'We need a solicitor—'

Elvi was thinking hard and fast but coming up with nothing. Her brain was still in shock. She wished she didn't know as much about her mother's fabulously wealthy employer as she did. He was the guy with the colour-coded closets and alphabetically arranged books. He had a desk that must never be touched and a bed that had to be changed every day. Her mother's duties in his apartment were hedged in by a very detailed list of do's and don'ts. That in the flesh the same male looked as though he had stepped straight out of a glossy magazine advertisement as a supermodel for designer apparel had struck Elvi as uniquely unfair.

She had read up about her mother's employer on the Internet, learning more that had made her grind her teeth together. *Why?* Because, Xan Ziakis seemed to have been born under a very lucky star, blessed by every conceivable attribute, and all he seemed to have learned from his remarkable good fortune was a marked tendency to behave as though he suffered from obsessive-compulsive disorder. Of course, maybe he did, she allowed ruefully, because nobody could possibly be that perfect in the real world. When she was still meeting her mother out of work to accompany her to AA meetings, she had seen Xan Ziakis coming home on several occasions while she sat waiting in the foyer of the luxury apartment block. And he was gorgeous to look at, absolutely, unmistakably gorgeous.

'I did the only thing I could,' Sally Cartwright confided hours later as she sat with her adopted daughter in the bedroom they shared. In her forties, she was a slender brunette with anxious green eyes now lined and shadowed with strain.

'It wasn't the only thing,' Elvi argued in a low voice, neither of them wanting Daniel in the next room to overhear them. 'You could've told the truth, both of you—'

'And do you really think anyone would have *believed* us?' her mother demanded tearfully, her cynicism unhidden. 'We're poor and down on our luck. Why? Because *I* wrecked all our lives, brought us down from a normal happy family to *this*!'

'This', expressed by a shamed hand gesture, encompassed the grim surroundings of their council flat in a tower block. But it was the guilt infused by Sally's bitten-back sob that worried Elvi the most, fearful as she was that her mother's distress would drive her back to alcohol. She knew better than to fall into reasoned argument with her mother on the score of her culpability because essentially the older woman was stating the unlovely truth.

At the time of Elvi's father's sudden death, the Cartwright family had been financially secure. They had owned their home and Sally had been a respected teacher in a girls' school but alcohol and a tide of growing debt had washed that safe, comfortable life away. Inevitably, Sally had lost her job and Elvi had left school at sixteen to find work. Like bricks tumbling down in a child's game, everything they had once taken for granted had been taken from them until they'd reached rock bottom and became homeless.

From there it had been a slow climb back to

security, a *very* slow climb, Elvi acknowledged wryly, but until this theft incident occurred their lives had steadily been improving. The three of them had rejoiced the day Daniel was accepted into medical school because it had been the first positive event they had had to celebrate in a very long time. Sally was so proud that, in spite of all that they had lost, Daniel had kept on studying and finally won through against such stiff competition because places to study medicine were very much oversubscribed in the UK. The threat of Daniel being ruined by one foolish mistake *could* destroy her mother all over again, Elvi thought with a sick sinking sensation in her stomach.

'No,' Sally declared steadily, her troubled face set with strong determination. 'This is *my* moment to make a sacrifice for everything *I* took from the two of you years ago and nothing you can say or do will change my mind on that score.'

Well, we'll just see about that, Elvi thought

defiantly as she lay in her bed that night, listening to her mother toss and turn, as unable to find sleep as her daughter. The mother she loved as much as she loved her little brother. Yet *her* mother had been her father's first wife, a Finnish nurse, tragically mown down by a car in a hospital car park within months of Elvi's birth. Her father had met and married Sally when Elvi was two years old and Elvi had no memories whatsoever of her birth mother. Her Scandinavian background came down to some faded photos and a handful of letters from an elderly Finnish grandma, who had died while she was still a child. For Elvi, family meant everything and she truly wished that her mother would accept that she and Daniel had long since forgiven her for her blunders.

After all, it wasn't as though Sally had *wanted* to become an alcoholic. Shattered by the sudden death of the husband she had adored, left alone to raise a six-year-old and a toddler, Sally had fallen apart in the grip of her grief and had slid into addiction by using alcohol as a crutch. Sally had had no other relatives to turn to for support and no close friends either because shortly before her husband's death, he had moved them all across the country to accept a new job. No, Elvi had sufficient compassion and understanding not to blame her mother for all their woes, nor was she willing to stand by and watch Sally undo all the progress she had made in recent years.

But realistically, what *could* she do?

Go and speak to Xan Ziakis in the hope that there was a streak of mercy beneath that designer suit and that frightening reputation for ruthless aggression and financial self-aggrandisement? Some hope, she mused wretchedly, feeling horribly weak and small and powerless. Xan Ziakis was feared in the City of London for his refusal to ever play as one of a team and his disdain for alliances, temporary or otherwise. He worked alone and her mother had never seen any evidence of a woman having been in his penthouse. Maybe he was gay…

No, not him, Elvi decided, shifting quietly beneath her duvet, remembering with shame a period when she had been almost obsessed by a need to see him daily. She didn't like to think about it but a sort of juvenile crush had engulfed her when she first saw Xan Ziakis. Not before time, she told herself drily; after all, life might have been all swings and not much roundabout throughout her unsettled and unhappy adolescence, but she was now twenty-two years old even if she was still almost as innocent as a child. Even so, she still recalled the single scorching appraisal Xan Ziakis had given her months ago and the flame that had leapt through her like a soaring torch along with the surprise of its effects on her body. No, he definitely wasn't gay, she was convinced. But the shock had been that a man who looked as he did could look at *her* that way.

She was no show-stopping beauty and she

bore not the smallest resemblance to the giraffe-legged bone-thin models she had seen on his arm in images on the Internet. Five feet two inches tall, she had white-blonde hair down to her waist, blue eyes and the sort of generous curves that made buying clothes a nightmare. She kept her hair long because the unusual colour was the one thing she liked about herself. As for the big breasts, the overly large bottom and the thick thighs, anyone was welcome to them. If only she had been the gym-bunny type, she reflected, but she hated gyms, hated dieting, hated getting on the scales and loved her food far too much. He must have been looking at the boobs, she thought ruefully.

Would the boobs get her into his presence? Embarrassed by her own thoughts, she winced, but she wasn't in a position to be precious about what it might take to get a meeting with Xan Ziakis. He was a very powerful, influential and wealthy man, whose staff probably guarded access to him as if he were a solid platinum trophy to be seen only by the fortunate and equally rich and important few. So, approach him at home? Or at his office?

He was way too private in his lifestyle to be approached at his penthouse. It would have to be the office. Shortly before dawn when Sally had fallen into a restless sleep, Elvi crept out of bed, having finally decided what to do next. Since she doubted the likelihood of Xan being willing to grant her a personal interview, she would write him a letter, telling him what she needed to say. It was worth a try, she thought limply, and better than doing nothing. *Only just*, her intelligence warned her.

On Daniel's laptop, she began to tell their family history, but only after humbly apologising for both troubling Xan and the theft. She wished it had been possible to tell him the truth but, like her mother, she reckoned it would be too dangerous to put Daniel back in the suspect corner. If she told Xan Ziakis the truth, he could easily drop the charges against her mother and instead pursue her brother and, even worse, he could then use the very letter she was writing against her family. Maybe writing *anything* down on paper was too dangerous, she thought fearfully, stopping in her task several times with a chill on her skin as she tried not to envisage even worse consequences coming their way.

But what other option did she have? Appealing to a man who might well have no heart was the only road she could take, and only then, if he was willing to see her, would she see him and plead her family's case to the best of her ability. Having to lie and state that her mother must have succumbed to an inexcusable moment of temptation distressed Elvi, but since Sally had already owned up to the theft with the police she didn't have much choice. She begged him to drop the charges because he had got his valuable artefact back. Did Xan Ziakis have any compassion? Was it possible that a man who had so much could be decent enough to be human and caring too?

The letter in an envelope squarely marked 'private and confidential' in one corner, Elvi waited on the pavement outside the Ziakis headquarters at eight that same morning. An assistant in a craft shop, she didn't start work until nine. And, according to her mother's idle chatter over the months, Xan Ziakis had a schedule that ran like clockwork. He left the penthouse at eight and travelled by limousine to his office seven days a week. *Seven*, she reflected wryly, a man who worked every day of the week for his success. Well, she could hardly criticise his work ethic.

The big black limousine drew up. The driver only opened the door after another car drew up behind and four men in dark suits sprang out. Looking on in dismay, Elvi registered that Xan Ziakis was guarded by a ring-of-steel protection before he even got a polished shoe out of his limo. Even so, she moved forward, her legs turning strangely wobbly as Xan himself emerged into daylight, blue-black hair gleaming like polished silk, his flawless bronzed cheek-bones taut below dark deep-set eyes, his lean, powerful body encased in an elegant suit that fitted him like a second skin, and there she froze.

'Get back!' someone said to her and, disconcerted, she retreated several steps still clutching her envelope.

Her quarry stalked on into the building…out of sight, *out of reach*, and she felt sick with failure, her face drained of colour, her eyes bleak.

A man appeared in front of her then, an older man, and there was something vaguely familiar about his craggy face. 'Is that letter you're gripping about your mother?' he asked bluntly. 'I work for Mr Ziakis too—'

'Oh,' Elvi said, taken aback by his approach. 'Yes, it's about Mum—'

'Then give it to me,' he urged. 'I'll see that it reaches the boss's desk.'

In a daze Elvi looked up and saw the kindness in his gaze. 'You're—?'

'Dmitri,' he supplied, twitching the letter out of her loosening grasp. 'I know your mother. I can't promise that the boss will read it or anything but I *can* put it on the desk.'

Elvi blinked. 'Thank you very much,' she murmured with warmth.

'No problem. She's a lovely lady,' Dmitri told her, walking off again at speed and vanishing into the building while tucking her letter into a pocket.

And Dmitri, whoever he is, doesn't think Sally Cartwright's a thief, Elvi realised as she climbed on a bus to get to work and mulled over that surprising encounter. Just as well, considering that she had frozen like an ice sculpture when she saw Xan Ziakis, not that she thought his bodyguards would have allowed her anywhere near him, because someone had told her to get out of the way. Dmitri? One of the other three men?

It didn't matter, she decided as she stocked shelves of knitting wool at work. The letter might land on Xan's desk but, as Dmitri had said, that didn't mean he would actually bother to read it or even more crucially respond to it.

But in that Elvi was mistaken. Xan was so disconcerted by the unexpected sight of his head of security covertly sliding an envelope onto his desk, when Dmitri clearly thought he was unseen, that nothing would have kept him from opening up that letter out of sheer human curiosity. Xan skimmed down to the signature first: *Elvi Cartwright*. He knew that name well enough and he also knew he should've been prepared for the tactic in such a situation. Instantly he wanted to crumple the letter up and bin it without reading it. That would have been the cautious way to deal.

Even so, although Xan was *very* cautious with women, he couldn't bring himself to dump the letter unread. A couple of months ago, he had noticed her, well, really, *really* noticed her, he acknowledged grimly, and he had instructed Dmitri to find out who she was, assuming that she lived in the same apartment block. He had, however, learned that she was his maid's daughter, which had naturally concluded his interest. Billionaires did not consort with the daughters of their domestic staff. The gulf was too immense, the risk of a messy affair too great.

And yet, all the same…the letter still unread, Xan drifted momentarily into the past, recalling Elvi Cartwright with intense immediacy. The shining pale-as-milk hair, the wonderful blue eyes, the crazy natural glow of her, not to mention the extraordinary fact that she looked very different from the sort of women he usually slept with and yet, inexplicably, one glance at her turned him on harder and faster than any of them.

She was a bit overweight, he supposed abstractedly; hard to tell when he had only ever seen her in a loose black jacket that swamped her. Very short in stature, not his type, absolutely *not* his type, he told himself sternly as he shook out the letter, more concerned by Dmitri's bizarre involvement in its delivery than by what it might say. If he couldn't trust his head of security, who could he trust? Why had Dmitri got personally involved in so tawdry an incident?

Xan had a scientific approach to everything he read. Elvi's use of English was far superior to what he would have expected and then he began reading and what he read was most educational from his point of view even if, by the end of it, he couldn't think why she expected *him as the victim* to want to do anything about Sally Cartwright's self-induced predicament.

Inevitably he studied the situation from his side of the fence, where all the power lay, and the sort of ideas that had never occurred to Xan Ziakis before when it came to a woman began very slowly to blossom. Xan, who never ever allowed himself to succumb to any kind of unwise temptation. Xan, who usually policed his every thought, suppressing any immoral promptings to concentrate more profitably on work. And once he let those bad ideas out of the box they created a positive riot in his imagination, raising the kind of excitement that only a good financial killing usually gave him…and that was it, Xan Ziakis was seduced by erotic possibilities for the first time in his life.

Xan folded the letter with a dark forbidding smile that his opponents would have recognised as a certain sign of danger and threat. He would give his quarry a couple of days to stew and wonder and *then* he would get in touch…

CHAPTER TWO

Two ANXIOUS DAYS in which she never allowed her phone to stray from her pocket passed for Elvi and on the third day, at the point where she had almost given up hope entirely, it finally rang.

One of Xan Ziakis's staff invited her to a meeting late that afternoon. Distracted by what lay ahead of her, she pleaded a dental appointment with her employer to finish early and worked over her usual lunch break instead. She got through her working hours on autopilot while anxiously rehearsing speeches in the back of her brain, only to discard them again when she tried to picture herself saying such things to a stranger. She would have to be lucid and brief, she told herself, because Xan Ziakis was unlikely to give her more than ten minutes of his time.

Seated in the plush quiet waiting area on the top floor of Ziakis Finance, Elvi was a bundle of nerves. How likely was it that he would even consider dropping the theft charge? Very unlikely, she reckoned, because what would be in that for him? But he *could* be a really good person, a little voice whispered. What were the chances? her brain scoffed, unimpressed by such wishful thinking. Xan was a merciless financier renowned for his profit margins. Every single thing he did during his working day was focused on gaining an advantage...and what did she have to offer?

She plucked a piece of tapestry wool off a black-trousered knee and shed her jacket to reveal the long-sleeved blue tee below because she was too warm. It was a waste of time approaching the wretched man when she was already virtually drowning in a sense of defeat, she told herself furiously. He was a rich, privileged guy, who lived a life far beyond the imagination of other, more ordinary mortals. He would not understand where she was coming from unless he had a reformed alcoholic in his own family circle. He would not appreciate the challenges Sally Cartwright had already overcome in her efforts to rebuild her life, nor could he even begin to imagine the misery of the 'lost' years that Elvi and Daniel had lived through with their mother.

Stop it, stop with the negative inner talk, she urged herself just as the svelte receptionist uttered her name in the same low-pitched tone that everyone who worked on the top floor seemed to use. Elvi rose stiffly from her seat, full of apprehension but struggling to appear composed because she knew that that was necessary. She couldn't afford to get emotional with such a self-disciplined man.

In his office, Xan was on a high because he was *finally* getting to meet *her*. The woman he had wanted, the *only* woman he had wanted in years that he couldn't have, but now that her mother was no longer his employee, and that connection was at an end, he no longer had to consider that aspect. That was done, dusted, in the past as far as he was concerned. Now he could move forward freely. Admittedly she was still of much lower status than he or her predecessors in his life had been but did he really have to be so particular about the women he took to his bed? He straightened his jacket and leant back against his designer desk as the door opened.

The office was the size of a football pitch, probably supposed to intimidate, Elvi decided, inching in from the doorway like a mouse trying to evade a hungry cat before she threw back her shoulders, straightened her back and lifted her chin, determined not to appear either weak or too humble.

'I'm Elvi, Sally Cartwright's daughter,' she declared quietly, battling to stand her ground as Xan Ziakis angled up his arrogant dark head, his classic nose as high as his perfect cheekbones to look directly at her.

Behind her the door closed, locking them into uneasy silence. Involuntarily Elvi connected with dazzling amber-gold eyes screened by criminally long and distinctive lush black lashes. She had never been close enough to him to see those eyes before, nor had she realised quite how tall he was, while even his formal business suit failed to conceal the power in his wide shoulders and muscular torso, not to mention the virile strength of his long thighs as he stood braced against his desk. He was drop-dead beautiful and at that moment she wasn't at all surprised that for a little while she had succumbed to a pathetically juvenile crush on him. She'd been far from being a teenager, and that crush had mortified her pride.

'Xander Ziakis,' he matched, extending an elegant lean brown hand.

At least he had manners, Elvi conceded feebly as she advanced to shake that hand, finding his grasp warm and her own cold with nerves, goose flesh erupting beneath her top as nervous tension threatened again. That close to him she could hardly breathe as a faint tang of some exotic designer cologne infiltrated her nostrils.

'Take a seat, Elvi,' he instructed, angling his head in the direction of the chair in front of him.

'I don't think I would be comfortable sitting down while you're still standing,' Elvi confided, stepping back but avoiding the chair, wondering if he was always as domineering, deciding he very probably was when she caught the flash of surprise in his gaze before he cloaked it. She reckoned everyone did exactly what they were told in his radius.

Disconcertingly and with a gleam of humour lightening his dark eyes, for he was rarely challenged, Xan slid back behind his desk and waited for her to sit down as he had told her to do.

Outmanoeuvred, Elvi took a seat and rested her bag on her lap to hide her trembling hands.

'Would you like a drink? Tea? Coffee? Water?' Xan proffered politely.

'Some water if it's not too much trouble,' Elvi framed, watching as he pressed a button and gave an order to some employee. Thirty seconds later, a moisture-beaded tumbler of water was clutched between her restive hands and she sipped, wetting her dry lips.

Xan studied her in fascination, because she was much more controlled than he had expected and possibly ten times more attractive close up than he had forecast. In reality he had been prepared for disappointment, having only seen her so fleetingly in the past. But there she was in front of him with skin that had the natural lustre of a pearl, eyes as blue as the Greek sky, dainty features and white-blonde hair falling like a cloak to her waist. And then there were the fabulous hourglass curves with that tiny waist, the amazing feminine bounty at breast and hip she had hidden beneath that awful coat. Not overweight, *glorious*, Xan decided hungrily, wondering if it would even occur to her that he had been forced to sit down because her body made him hot as hell. He thought not, for there was nothing even slightly flirtatious or inviting about either her clothing or her attitude, and he wasn't accustomed to that lack of interest in the women he met. This one hadn't even bothered to put on make-up, he registered in mounting surprise.

'Why do you think I offered you this appointment?' Xan enquired with innate ruthlessness, because he doubted his reading of her character from her appearance and behaviour. He didn't trust women. He had *learned* not to trust women through the experience of growing up with several unpleasant stepmothers and the conviction had been rubber-stamped by his first love's change of heart the instant she realised his family fortune was gone.

'I don't know, which is why I am here,' Elvi said truthfully. 'Obviously you read my letter—'

Xan lounged back in his chair and lightly

shifted an eloquent brown hand as if in dismissal of the letter. 'Why would I want to do anything for a woman who stole from me?' he asked bluntly.

In receipt of that acerbic enquiry, Elvi lost colour. 'Well, maybe not *want*—'

'That's the problem,' Xan interposed before she could even finish speaking. 'I don't want to help her because I believe that those who break the law should be punished—'

'Yes, *but*—' Elvi began afresh, thrown on the back foot because before her mother had been charged with theft she would have agreed with him on that score.

'There is no saving exception in my book,' Xan Ziakis sliced in again. 'I felt more sorry for you growing up with an alcoholic parent than I feel sorry for her.'

Elvi's hands tightened around the glass cradled between her hands and she forced herself to sip again; she wanted to slap him and shut him up because he wasn't allowing her to get in a word in her mother's defence. 'We don't need your compassion!' she heard herself snap back and then she bit her lip hard, knowing she shouldn't have responded in that tone for there was truth in that old adage about catching more flies with honey than vinegar.

'But *you* chose to *ask* for my compassion,' Xan reminded her with dogged purpose. 'And I have to wonder, what's in it for me?'

'You have your jade pot back?' Elvi suggested shakily.

'But I don't. It's police evidence at this moment in time,' Xan told her gently.

Elvi breathed in deep and slow, battling to think straight while he sat there as cool as a block of untouchable ice, and then she clashed with eyes that flamed over her like a fire and realised that his apparently glacial outlook had given her a mistaken impression of him. For a split second as her chest swelled on that breath, his gaze had dropped revealingly below her chin and she was shaken that he could be quite as predictable as most of the men she met. Her boobs were playing more of a starring role than *she* was, she thought bitterly.

'My mother *has* been punished,' Elvi argued, taking another tack in her growing desperation. 'She's been arrested and that was frightening for her and more than enough to teach most people a hard lesson. She has also lost her job and her good name—'

'*Elvi...*' Xan leant across his desk to interrupt her again.

'No, don't cut me off this time!' Elvi urged impatiently. 'Tell me why you can't drop the charges—'

'I've already answered that question,' Xan reminded her with finality.

Enormous blue eyes fixed on him hopefully. 'But don't you think that making a benevolent gesture would make you feel good?'

Xan could not believe how naïve she was and he almost laughed. 'I don't have a benevolent bone in my body,' he admitted without embar-rassment. 'I'm a hard-hitter. That's who I am.'

'Well, I didn't come here to repeat the sob story I already put in my letter,' Elvi assured him with cringing dignity as she started rising from her seat. 'So, if that's your last word—'

'It's not. You don't listen very well, do you?' Xan shot back at her in exasperation. 'I asked you what would be in this benevolent gesture for me and I do *have* an option to offer you—'

Taken aback at the very point where she had felt that she was getting nowhere with him, Elvi sank slowly back into the chair. 'You…er…do?' she queried dubiously, her eyes openly bemused by the concept.

'It's simple and unscrupulous,' Xan warned her without hesitation. 'I want you. Give your-self to me and I will drop the charges.'

Elvi's lower lip parted company with the upper one as she stared back at him in complete as-tonishment, not quite willing to believe he had actually said those words to her. *Give yourself to me.* He meant sex. What else could he mean? *I want you.* The most enormous sense of shock engulfed her. It wasn't simply unscrupulous, it was filthy, and she was shattered that he could sit there behind his rule-the-world desk and dare to offer her such an offensive escape clause on her mother's behalf. What world did he live in? What kind of women was he accustomed to dealing with? It was a horrific suggestion no decent woman would accept.

'I finally appear to have silenced you,' Xan remarked with unhidden amusement.

And it was that glint of amusement in his extravagantly handsome face and the energy of it in his accented intonation that set free the tide of rage inside Elvi. She flew upright like a rocket and her hand jerked up and she flung the glass of water over him. 'How dare you?' she snapped at him furiously. 'I'm not a slut!'

Xan shook his dark head, water droplets rolling down his lean, dark, dangerous face. Never had he been attacked in such a way, but it didn't show because he did not move a single muscle. He gazed broodingly back at her, disturbed by her passionate nature but already wondering how that seeming flaw would play out between his sheets. Obviously he was bored with the identikit mistresses who had met his physical needs for years, but that rational, unemotional approach worked for him, he reminded himself, staving off the risks of more personal entanglements. 'I didn't suggest that you were, but there's a vacancy in my bed at present and I would be happy for you to fill it for a couple of months—'

'Well, I wouldn't be happy to fill it!' Elvi snarled back incredulously. 'A *vacancy*? Is that how you think of sex?'

'It is a need like hunger, an appetite that must be met,' Xan responded levelly, his hard, dark gaze locked to hers like a laser beam that made her body as hot and perspiring as if she were under a spotlight. 'If it makes you feel better, I wanted you the first time I saw you waiting in the foyer of my apartment block. I found out your name then and your connection to my maid. Doing anything about the attraction would've been inappropriate at that time—'

Elvi studied him in helpless wonderment. 'I don't believe this… I don't believe any of it!' she gasped. 'You don't even know me—'

Xan lounged back in his seat, damp but disciplined. 'I don't need to *know* you to want to have sex with you. I'm more about the physical than the cerebral with women,' he admitted smoothly.

'But you're trying to buy me with a bribe!' Elvi condemned furiously.

'And if the offer suits you, I'll drop the theft charge. That's how negotiations work in this world, Elvi. *You* give, *I* give. It really is that basic—'

'But it's blackmail!' Elvi accused heatedly, increasingly unnerved by his shattering level of inhuman self-control.

'No, it's not. You have a choice. Whether you

choose to accept my offer or not is entirely up to you,' Xan pointed out with precision. 'Think it over for a week…'

'I'm not going to think it over!' Elvi assured him with blazing conviction. 'It's a filthy proposition and I'm not that sort of woman—'

'Presumably you enjoy sex like other women,' Xan interposed very drily. 'If you're afraid that I might be into something different like BDSM, you're wrong. I'm completely normal in the sex department—'

'I don't care! I'm not interested in what you do in the bedroom!' Elvi proclaimed, pacing his office carpet in a passion of disbelief at the direction their interview had gone in, her triangular face as red as a tomato. 'I couldn't imagine being some sort of sex slave—'

Xan laughed out loud, shocking her again, startling her as he sprang up from behind his desk and extended a business card to her. 'The word you seek is mistress, *not* sex slave, which is rather melodramatic, if you don't mind me saying so—'

'Yes, I *do* mind!' Elvi gasped, snatching the card off him and backing away at speed from his proximity, her heart beating so fast she feared it might bounce right out of her tight chest. 'I mind every darned thing you've said since I arrived. I didn't like any of it and I wouldn't have come to this meeting if I'd known you were likely to suggest some immoral arrangement to me! Call me stupid but that idea didn't even cross my mind!'

Xan had never wanted to touch a woman as badly as he did at that moment. *Thee mou...* she excited him to the most extraordinary degree. Her amazing chest was heaving, her blue eyes were huge with anxiety and her opulent pink pouty mouth was yet another temptation that tugged at him as he pictured her lying in his bed. It was lust of the lowest possible order, he acknowledged grimly, but somehow, even though lust had never driven him to such a degree and he thoroughly distrusted the urge, he couldn't shake free of it. The harder she argued with him, the more he wanted to persuade her because, whatever else Elvi Cartwright was, she was neither boring nor insipid. A sex slave though, he savoured with unholy amusement, even while he wondered if that could possibly be a fantasy of hers...how did he know? But he very badly wanted to know about *her* fantasies. Yet he could not recall ever being so curious about any other woman and his innate caution cut in.

She was saying no, shrieking no, in fact, and possibly that was for the best, he reasoned flatly even as all the potential colour and enjoyment drained straight back out of his immediate future again. Was he so bored with his life that he had proposed such an innovative exchange of favours? It was out of character for him. He picked up women and dropped them again as easily as he worked seven days a week. He didn't normally *picture* them in that apartment bed, he merely joined them there to satisfy a natural desire for physical satisfaction.

'You have my phone number if you change your mind,' Xan Ziakis intoned, as if he could not quite credit that she had turned him down.

Elvi tossed her head, platinum-blonde hair spilling across her shoulders. She would have made a terrific Lady Godiva, Xan reflected abstractedly, wondering why he was even thinking that. He stalked across to the door and opened it for her, now determined to bring the unsettling meeting to a quick conclusion.

'Good luck,' he murmured graciously, feeling inordinately proud of himself for his restraint.

Blue eyes collided with his. 'You are the most hateful man I have ever met!' she hissed at him like a cat flexing her sharp claws and, turning on her heel, she sped off down the corridor.

Xan noted that she had left her jacket behind, lifted it and strode out of his office again.

'Elvi!' he called when he saw her standing

at the lift, hugging her handbag as if it were a comforter.

Eyes flying wide, she spun and he handed her the jacket.

'Oh…thanks,' she mumbled in disconcertion, suddenly uncomfortably aware that every employee in the area had stilled to watch them.

That was the instant when Xan saw the tears glimmering in her eyes and wished he hadn't followed her. It made him feel like an ogre who kicked puppies, a complete bastard. But he was what he was and he had never been soft in heart or deed, he reasoned harshly. She needed to toughen up because the world was a thoroughly nasty place.

Still shell-shocked by that encounter with Xan, Elvi went home and found her mother in tears at the kitchen table. 'I don't know how I'm going to get work anywhere without a reference from my last job,' she confided chokily. 'And I can't tell the truth either. Nobody wants a light-fingered employee!'

Elvi paled. 'We'll think up something,' she said soothingly. 'Is Daniel at the restaurant?'

'Yes. Thank goodness he got that bar job. At least it gets him out of his room,' his mother remarked unhappily. 'He's so depressed, Elvi. He feels so guilty—'

Elvi nodded, trying not to think that, had she been of a different persuasion, she might have been able to make the whole nightmare go away. It would be indecent, though, for her to have sex with Xan Ziakis in return for him dropping the theft charge. Totally disgustingly indecent, she told herself squarely. Surely she didn't have to sink *that* low to help her family?

She lay awake half the night thinking about it. The irony was that before she had met Xan Ziakis he was the only man she had ever thought of having sex with. Well, in her dreams, her imagination, that was, because he was the first man she had ever been strongly attracted to. Of course, she had met very few men. Few men went into craft shops; customers who liked to knit, crochet and embroider were mostly of the female persuasion, although not exclusively. Throughout most of her teen years, while other young girls were flirting and dating, Elvi had been looking after her little brother and tucking her comatose mother into bed at night. She had missed out on a large chunk of her supposedly carefree youth, having to be responsible, having to be the adult for as long as Sally had been incapable of meeting that challenge.

By the way, I'm still a virgin, she tried to picture herself telling Xan Ziakis. Unexpectedly, her body shook with sudden laughter at the image. No doubt Xan had assumed that she was experienced when he'd made that crack about women enjoying sex as well. No doubt he also believed she would be mistress material with the sort of sexy tricks a more practised lover would provide. But she had no tricks, no clue, *nothing* to give in that department, and she was quite sure that that would have disillusioned him, maybe even put him off.

Although, how would that have helped them? He had only made that ridiculous offer because he found her attractive. For a split second, she cherished the knowledge of that startling truth. Xan Ziakis found *her* attractive as well. It was a fact that bolstered her ego even though she knew it shouldn't. Probably the boobs again, she thought wryly. As an adolescent, who had been tormented at school by the boys once she began developing way beyond what she had deemed an acceptable size, she had always loathed her large breasts and ample hips. Joel, her best mate since primary school, told her she looked lush and feminine, but then that was exactly the sort of comforting comment a friend was supposed to make, so she hadn't paid any heed to it.

The following morning, Joel sent her a text asking her to meet him at lunchtime. She smiled at the prospect, knowing she could tell her friend the truth about her mother and her brother, although she had no intention of mentioning Xan's proposition.

'How could a boy as smart as Daniel be that dumb?' Joel demanded, smoking while they sat outside a bar close to where she worked.

'Clever people don't always have common sense,' Elvi pointed out, leaning across the table to add, 'You're getting eyed up by that beautiful blonde over there. I think it's time I went back to work—'

'No!' Joel protested, closing an imprisoning hand over the one she had braced on the table-top to rise. 'I'm not interested—'

'You haven't even looked yet,' Elvi rebuked as she met his brown eyes and wondered how his could be so different from Xan's, because they did not make her melt or heat up to even the smallest degree. Yet, Joel was tall and attractive with tousled dark curls. He was also an up-and-coming successful painter, already being singled out for his talent with portraits. But then Joel's life had gone much more smoothly than her own, she reflected ruefully, and sometimes she marvelled that he still stayed in touch with her because they now led such divergent lives.

'All I want to do right now is give you some cash to help out,' Joel told her ruefully. 'You earn a pittance and with Sally out of work—'

'No, thanks,' Elvi cut in hastily. 'Thanks for offering but no, thanks—'

'Don't you ever just want to walk away from the two of them and their problems?' her friend enquired ruefully. 'You could've been so much *more* without them holding you back—'

'You're talking about my mother and my brother,' Elvi reminded him tartly. 'I love them and they love me and you don't turn your back on that kind of love and support—'

'But you're always supporting *them*, not yourself!' Joel argued.

He didn't understand, he never *had* understood, Elvi reflected wryly, because his was not a close family. Elvi, however, knew that, no matter what happened to her, her mother and her brother would always be there for her just as she was for them. That made her feel warm and complete inside herself in a way she couldn't have described even to her longest-standing friend.

'I'm wasting my breath,' Joel recognised impatiently as Elvi slid back into her black jacket. 'For some bizarre reason you don't want the stuff other women want…the new clothes, the parties, the *fun*—'

'I'd give anything to own a dog,' she confided, and not for the first time.

'A dog would just be another burden,' Joel reproved.

Didn't stop her wanting one, Elvi reasoned wryly as she got off the bus to go home that evening. A dog to walk and cuddle when she felt lonely. A cat was a possibility but cats weren't necessarily cuddly, being more independent. As usual the lift was out of service and she had to climb flight after flight of stairs to the tenth floor, telling herself all the while that the exercise was keeping her fit even if she was wheezing like an old lady by the time she walked into the kitchen. That lighter mood didn't last once she saw her mother and brother standing there, clearly in the middle of a rare argument.

'What's wrong?' she asked tightly.

'Look, what I did wrecked everything for *all* of us,' Daniel declared forthrightly. 'Mum can't find work now, and you hardly earn anything. How are we going to live? Obviously I have to find a *permanent* job—'

'No, that's not what this is all about,' Elvi cut in hastily. 'That would make what Mum did pointless, Daniel. We *want* you to go to university and train to be a doctor—'

'I did this. This is *my* responsibility and I'm old enough to behave like a man,' her little but very tall baby brother announced. 'A man doesn't turn his back on his family and just go off and become a student without thinking about how *they* are going to survive!'

Elvi thought a very rude word inside her head,

her shoulders slumping, and passed on by into the bedroom to sink down on her bed. Daniel was like a mule when he set his heart on anything and now he too was in full sacrificial mode, just like her mother. What now? If Daniel threw away his chance, it wouldn't come around again, and if he did that Sally Cartwright would self-destruct because her son going to medical school was the one thing she had in life to focus on and be proud of.

Xan Ziakis had won, Elvi reflected wretchedly, because her family was falling apart before her very eyes. From the kitchen she could hear the distressing noise of her mother and her brother having a major row as Sally tried to dissuade him from his plans and he fought back loudly. She pulled the business card out of her bag and reached for her phone. She didn't want to speak to a man she hated, a man who was forcing her into a choice that went against everything she had ever valued, so she texted him instead.

Rethink on mistress as you forecast. Need to discuss conditions of servitude.

Across London, Xan checked his phone and laughed out loud, something he didn't do very often and which spooked him with its unfamiliarity. He had won. He *always* won, he reminded himself with satisfaction. But even so there was a sweeter taste to this victory than most.

Meet you for dinner at eight...

And he gave her the address, telling her to ask for *his* table.

CHAPTER THREE

ELVI WENT INTO her slender wardrobe to withdraw a pair of black velour leggings and a black, rather glittery festive top she had received for Christmas the year before. The outfit would have to do because she didn't have anything else to wear.

'Where on earth are you going dressed like that?' Sally Cartwright demanded boldly as her daughter passed through the kitchen, wearing actual lip gloss and mascara to her mother's wonderment.

'I've got a date for dinner,' Elvi admitted, having reasoned that she had to make a start on her cover story.

'A...*date*?' her mother exclaimed in astonishment.

'Yes, he's handsome, he's rich, he can give

me a good time, what's not to like?' she asked the older woman wryly. 'I'm twenty-two and I never go out. Isn't it time I got a life?'

'Of course, it is,' Sally agreed uneasily. 'I was only surprised, not questioning you.'

'I don't know if I'll be back tonight,' Elvi announced uncomfortably, her face flaming, but she had to work on her cover story.

'Elvi...?' her mother pronounced in a shaken tone, but she compressed her lips and said nothing more, accepting that her daughter was an adult woman.

Only Elvi felt nothing like an adult woman as she entered an exclusive restaurant, maddeningly conscious that she was underdressed, and where she was looked up and down in open dismissal before the mention of Xan's name produced a very different reaction and suddenly she was 'Madam...' and being escorted by the head waiter to the promised table where Xan was already seated, perusing the extensive wine list.

Xan leapt upright. He was a four-letter word of

a man but someone some time had trained him well in courtesy, Elvi acknowledged, bending to set down her bag before deigning to take a seat in the chair pulled out for her occupation.

Xan was transfixed by his view of her. She was very poorly clothed, but the instant she bent down and he caught a glimpse of her rounded derriere outlined in clinging velour he became a spontaneous fan of clingy leggings that outlined the female form. A bottom as deliciously curvy and ripe as a peach met his attention and the stirring at his groin was even more immediate. He asked himself how he could possibly have reached thirty years of age without appreciating that he found curvaceous women more sexually appealing than their thinner cousins. Or was it only *her*? Something weird about her? That mane of long hair?

'Elvi,' he murmured in welcome. 'What would you like to drink?'

'I don't drink. Water, please,' she told him, settling into her seat, seemingly unaware that he was riveted to his, locked there by the equally clingy glittery top that showcased her breasts. The smooth pale expanse of soft firm flesh and only the merest hint of cleavage sent the pulse below his belt to throbbing discomfort and a level of arousal that set his even white teeth on edge, because he was neither a horny teenager nor a sex-starved man and anything excessive in any personal field set off Xan's caution alarm.

She didn't drink. That didn't bother Xan at all because he had had the experience of several women who liked to drink a little too much and turned into public embarrassments. An alcoholic in the family, he recalled; naturally she was careful. He ordered wine for himself and ordered meals for both of them, as was his habit with companions.

Elvi sipped her water and watched food selections she hadn't ordered brought to the table with great pomp and ceremony. She wasn't that surprised by his failure to offer her a personal choice or a menu. He was a control freak. He was accustomed to commanding what other people did, even, it seemed, what they *ate*. He would probably be hell in bed, she found herself thinking ruefully, imagining what that innate selfishness would translate to in terms of sex with another person. But then what did she know about it? Maybe that was the norm for a rich man like him. A woman of her status was simply a new toy for him to play with, nothing more.

Elvi cleared her throat awkwardly. 'So, this arrangement…how long would it last exactly?'

'Three months,' Xan heard himself declare, although he had never before mentioned anything longer than two. He was being practical, he told himself, ensuring he could keep her until he got bored, and he *could* get bored the very first month, couldn't he? That had happened on a couple of occasions and could well happen with her.

Elvi studiously stared down at her water. 'And how often…er, would I…*see* you?'

'I doubt if there's a virile man in the world who would answer that question in advance,' Xan quipped, amusement flashing through him as he wondered how many one-night stands she had enjoyed. At her age, that was the norm, wasn't it? Or was it? He had no idea because he had never made use of that kind of freedom, reluctant to follow in the footsteps of a father who had been a notorious womaniser and playboy. He had never slept around, never been attracted by indiscriminate casual sex with strangers.

Elvi reddened, heat coursing through her as she met brilliant dark eyes alive with the kind of powerhouse energy he had kept in abeyance during that interview in his office. Stupid question, she conceded uneasily, insanely aware of the tightening of her nipples and the bizarre flush of warmth rising from her pelvis. Both sensations were unhappily familiar, echoes of what she had felt every time she'd seen Xan walk past her months earlier. She hadn't known attraction could make her feel like that about a man and she hadn't appreciated the yearning sense of vulnerability it infused her with.

'I will provide you with an apartment and a new wardrobe. You need clothes,' Xan intoned with a casualness that shot her straight back out of her reverie.

An apartment. Elvi swallowed hard, reminding herself that it would only be for a few months and that she could hardly act the mistress while sharing a bedroom with her adoptive mother.

'Why do I need *you* to buy *me* clothes?' she queried rather sourly.

'When I need a partner to attend a social engagement, you will be my companion,' Xan informed her, startling her afresh because she had assumed that being a mistress was a very discreet role in a back room some place where she would be hidden from public view.

'Not sure I would be up to that challenge,' Elvi admitted ruefully. 'You live in a very exclusive world.'

'You would merely be on my arm,' Xan told

her as if she were a man bag. 'You wouldn't even need to speak. I would handle conversation—'

'Like you handled ordering my meal for me?' Elvi gently nudged her untouched plate away another few inches. 'If you had asked, I would've told you that I don't eat fish—'

'Fish is healthy,' Xan informed her smoothly.

'But you're not my doctor or my dietician and I am not so stupid that I require your guidance. I *hate* fish,' Elvi spelled out with emphatic cool.

Xan shrugged a broad shoulder, impervious to her reproof. 'So, order something else.'

'I'm really not hungry,' Elvi told him truthfully. 'As I said in my text, I'm only here to hear the conditions.'

'Of servitude,' Xan reminded her silkily. 'I *like* that word. It has a lovely medieval ring to it.' He removed something from an inside pocket and set it down beside her hand: it was a key with a label attached. 'The apartment key and the address. Do you require assistance to move in?'

'How soon will you withdraw the theft charge?' Elvi pressed anxiously. 'And no, no assistance required. I don't have much stuff.'

'The day you move in, the charge will be withdrawn,' Xan supplied. 'I will not do anything before that. You could still back out—'

Elvi tensed. 'And if I gave you my word of honour that I wouldn't?'

A cool smile curved his wide sensual lips. 'I wouldn't trust it. Women can be unpredictable—'

'As can men.' Elvi grasped the apartment key as though it were a stinging nettle and thrust it hurriedly into her bag. 'I'll move in tomorrow. What about my job?'

'You quit. When I want you, I naturally want you to be available,' Xan pointed out smoothly.

'I'll need to work a notice period,' she protested.

'No, you simply leave,' Xan contradicted arrogantly. 'From this moment on, you're my responsibility—'

Elvi froze as if he had struck her. 'Servitude is biting right now,' she conceded between gritted teeth. 'I don't like depending on anyone outside my family.'

'But now and first and foremost, you've got me and my demands to consider. I will deliver if you do,' Xan completed levelly. 'I will treat you like a princess.'

Yes, once upon a time, princesses had had to get into bed with strangers as well, Elvi thought mutinously, although at least they had been married off first. Not that she wanted to be married to him, which would probably be even worse than being *owned* by him, because that was how he was making her feel. Like a new possession, a *thing*, an object, rather than a person.

'I'm really not going to be very suitable for purpose,' she warned him tightly.

'Then you've been with the wrong men,' Xan assured her with unblemished confidence, his

flawless cheekbones slashing taut to accentu-
ate the brilliance of his stunning brown eyes
and their black lashes.

Her face burning at that recollection, Elvi
climbed into bed in the dark, striving not to
wake her mother up.

'Elvi…?' the older woman whispered. 'Did
you have a nice evening?'

Remembering her fib about having a date,
Elvi grimaced. 'Yes.' She hesitated and then
pressed ahead. 'I've been thinking of moving
out and in with a…er…a *flatmate*,' she selected
the final word abruptly.

Silence greeted her from her mother's direction and she wasn't surprised because she knew
that her sudden announcement would shock
Sally. Even more, though, did Elvi hate the necessity of telling lies because she knew that she
could not possibly tell the truth.

'Anyone I know?' Sally prompted.

'No. A friend of Joel's but if I want to move

in I have to move in tomorrow,' Elvi completed. 'I'm sorry it's such short notice—'

'No, don't apologise. You're twenty-two, Elvi, and naturally you would like some independence and freedom. I had those things at your age—why shouldn't you? Please don't sound so apologetic about it,' Sally Cartwright responded a shade shakily. 'You stayed with us all the years Daniel and I needed you, so, although I'll miss you, I'm certainly not about to try and make you change your mind.'

Relieved by that exchange, Elvi lay still until a tiny sniff alerted her to the reality that her mother was crying and she slid straight out of bed and wrapped her arms around the older woman as well as she could with the duvet separating them. 'I love you,' she framed, feeling ridiculously guilty about moving out even though she knew she didn't want to move but *had* to for Xan Ziakis's benefit.

'Things will settle down again. This is only a rough patch,' the older woman told her more cheerfully. 'I'll find work. Daniel will start classes and we'll all go back to normal again. We only have to be patient and strong.'

The next morning, Daniel accompanied Elvi to the Tube station with her single suitcase. 'You're moving in with a man, aren't you?' he shot unexpectedly at his sister, and when she glanced up with pink cheeks and a look of guilt, he laughed. 'Yeah, thought so. Mum's worried some smartass is taking advantage of you—'

'I'm not stupid,' Elvi declared, but saw no reason to add any further details when she was sure she would be moving back home again within a couple of months, if not sooner.

'Well, you *are* rushing into this too fast, but that's your business,' her sibling conceded, halting to pass her the case, which was too old to have handy wheels attached. 'Look after yourself, sis, and make sure you visit us when I'm not working.'

Tears were prickling in Elvi's eyes by the time

she boarded the train and she gave herself an urgent reality check, reminding herself of the theft charge that would be dropped and the sheer guilt and strain that would drop away and allow her mother and brother to continue their lives without further harm. It *would* be worth it, she told herself urgently, absolutely worth anything she had to do to achieve that desirable result.

The apartment in an elegant building overlooking the Thames was much larger and fancier than she had dimly expected. She wandered around barefoot on opulent marble floors, viewing the beautiful and immaculate living area with its leather sofas and contemporary paintings. She walked out onto the balcony to take in the busy view of the river before entering a kitchen equipped with every necessity as well as a fully stocked fridge and freezer. She marvelled at the two separate opulent bathrooms she discovered off the very spacious bedroom, as well as a dressing room fitted with loads of closet space. It was a property prepared for the sort of woman who took a great deal of interest in her appearance, she reasoned with raised brows, noting the number of mirrors and racks for shoes and handbags. She was starting to unpack her case when the doorbell pinged.

A svelte older woman carrying garment bags greeted her. 'I'm Sylvia. Mr Ziakis asked me to choose an outfit for you to wear tonight.'

So, it begins, Elvi acknowledged ruefully, her new life as an object. Xan hadn't bothered to tell her personally that he planned to take her somewhere that very evening and how had he even *known* she had moved in? Were there secret cameras installed? she wondered apprehensively.

'Nothing will be a perfect fit until I take your measurements,' Sylvia announced, unfurling a measuring tape. 'Could we take this into the bedroom? It would be more comfortable for you to try on the dresses I've brought for you to choose from.'

Elvi wasn't comfortable in any way having

to strip down to her underwear for a complete stranger but she compressed her lips and did what she had to do, barely pausing to glance at her reflection in blue dress after blue dress.

'Only blue?' she queried.

'Mr Ziakis specified blue,' she was told as Sylvia whisked the tape over her figure and jotted down measurements on her tablet. 'Seems to be his new favourite colour, at least for you—'

'You've done this before for him with other women, haven't you?' Elvi commented.

'Every service that my company offers Mr Ziakis is completely confidential,' Sylvia countered with perfect diplomacy.

Elvi wasn't listening. Xander Ziakis was evidently a serial womaniser, given to keeping mistresses whom he placed in an apartment and dressing them from head to toe in *his* choice of colour and fashion. She was appalled and soon wondering how many other women had lived in the apartment before her and whether he had cared in any way about a single one of them. When he had said he was more about the physical than the cerebral, he hadn't been joking. Her attention strayed to the vast divan bed she had studiously ignored since her arrival and she breathed in deep, striving not to think about the sex aspect.

After all, thinking about it wasn't going to make it go away and dwelling on something she couldn't avoid would be foolish. She tried on the half-dozen dresses and vanished into one of the bathrooms to find the right size for the fancy lingerie Sylvia had placed on the bed. She chose the dress that fitted the best and hid the most, not being a fan of her own cleavage. Her back and arms and legs would be on show and that was quite enough, in her opinion. She had to practise walking in the very high heeled sandals and they pinched her toes horribly. It was a very great shame that wearing a designer outfit that probably cost hundreds if not *thousands* of pounds had never been on her bucket list, she conceded ruefully.

What on earth did Xan want with a young woman like her? For goodness' sake, she was a shop girl, or had been until she'd quit earlier that day in a very uncomfortable phone call to her employer. She was ordinary, not special, not a beauty, no great wit. What did Xan see in her that was so desirable he would go to such lengths to have her?

She looked in the mirror. Her *body*—what a lowering thought that was, she reflected unhappily. He didn't know her, wouldn't waste time even *trying* to get to know her; he only wanted to have sex with her, and the fancy apartment and the ridiculously big wardrobe Sylvia had insisted she would need were simply the luxury trappings that she was expected to be delighted to receive. She had no doubt that other women had enjoyed those benefits from sharing their bodies with a very, very rich man but, unfortunately for her, she wasn't one of them. She felt cheapened by living in an apartment Xan owned, wearing clothes and eating food provided by him. It felt too much like being paid for sex. But that was the arrangement she had agreed to, she reminded herself, and she did not see that she could do much about it.

For the first time in over a year, when a bout of flu had forced him to deviate from his routine, Xan finished at the office early. He acknowledged that Elvi roused an unusual sense of excitement that was new to his experience. It was nothing he couldn't handle though, he thought, choosing to be amused by his mood rather than disturbed by it. She was new, she was fresh, there was nothing odd about his interest. He was a normal guy, his libido inflamed by the prospect of a different woman. He texted her the time she would be picked up and smiled.

Elvi was disconcerted when the bell went shortly before eight and she was confronted with Dmitri on the doorstep. 'Ready?' he asked flatly, somehow radiating disapproval in waves.

Her complexion flaming, Elvi dug her key into the fancy clutch that matched her ridiculous shoes and preceded him into the lift he had already had waiting for her. 'What's your job with Xan?' she enquired stiffly.

'I'm the head of his security team. Does Sally know about this?' he framed.

'Of course not,' Elvi parried uncomfortably. 'I don't want her to know either.'

The older man released his breath impatiently and said nothing more, but the attitude he emanated had left her in no doubt that he had guessed exactly what her new role in his employer's life was and she was mortified by the deep sense of shame that engulfed her.

'What's wrong?' Xan heard himself demand as soon as he saw her, because instead of the smile, the warmth that he had somehow vaguely expected from her, she was flushed and stiff as a waxwork with her usual glow absent.

'Nothing,' Elvi responded tightly.

'I hate it when people lie to me,' Xan told her warningly.

'Well, if you must know, I feel like the slut I

said I wasn't!' Elvi rounded on him helplessly, her emotions overpowering her innate practicality. 'Living in an apartment *you* own, wearing clothes *you* paid for!'

Never having been attacked on that score before, Xan tensed, slowly coming to terms with the truth that for the first time in his life he might just have chosen a woman with moral principles. He was utterly spooked by the suspicion. 'You're *not* a slut,' he breathed in a curt undertone of denial. 'We have an agreement—'

The reminder steadied Elvi as nothing else could have done. 'The theft charge?'

'Dropped. *Gone*,' Xan emphasised with relief, expecting that to improve her mood.

But Elvi said nothing, refusing to believe that assurance until she heard it from her mother herself. She knew Sally would have phoned her immediately with such news, not sat on it. Her hands merely tightened around her clutch.

'I have some jewellery for you to wear,' Xan continued.

'Don't want it,' she said mutinously.

'Nonetheless you *will* wear it as part of your role,' Xan contradicted, settling a wide shallow box on her lap without apology. 'You're being childish and difficult and that's not what I want from you.'

Possibly that was the wake-up call Elvi felt she needed at the moment. She *had* agreed to the mistress role and there was no room to wriggle out of the arrangement again. Gritting her teeth together, she opened the box on a diamond necklace and earrings that flashed like white fire as the streetlights illuminated the limo's interior. She pushed her hair over one shoulder and reached for the necklace but Xan got there before her.

'Allow me,' he breathed, tugging her round by the shoulder to put her back to him, so close to her that the sheer heat of his body hit her bare back like a burn inflicted by the sun and she froze as he bent over her to attach the necklace at her nape.

That close, he smelt amazing, a dynamite combination of clean, crisp masculinity, exotic cologne and an element that was uniquely his own but which reminded her of fresh air and the woods. The startling wonder of his scent filtered through her like an aphrodisiac, shocking her afresh. Her breath hitching in her dry throat, she shifted away again fast and fumbled for the earrings to attach them.

'You're very jumpy for a woman I have yet to touch,' Xan observed.

'This situation is new to me,' Elvi pointed out nervously.

'It's not a situation. It's a relationship like any other.' Xan surprised himself by saying the word he always avoided because he *knew* it wasn't a relationship, it was purely a sexual connection.

Now you're giving her mixed messages, he reproved himself immediately. No, he was simply trying to make her relax before she wrecked his good mood. He had set this up; he could hardly complain about her being different from the kind of women he was accustomed to when he had known that from the start. He was no softie with women but he was always rational, fair, he assured himself until he tried to apply that statement to the manner in which he had *acquired* Elvi, and the oddest sense of discomfiture assailed him for the first time ever in a woman's presence.

Elvi shot him an anxious glance, big blue eyes as easily read as a headline. There was a sort of strange innocence about her, almost as if she was expecting him to break out a whip and chains. Stubborn mouth quirking, he shelved that sudden unlikely suspicion, choosing instead to recall the moment she had looked back at him a couple of months back in the apartment foyer. She had wanted him then and he had known it, was way too experienced in that department with women to be mistaken. And now he had made it possible for her to *have* him and she ought to be pleased about that, shouldn't she? *He* was pleased. Why wasn't she? Why did women have to be so blasted irrational and changeable? And since when had he cared when one was? He was wasting way too much time speculating on her behaviour and it was inappropriate with a sexual partner.

He took her to a very exclusive party in a London town house with a man playing jazz at a grand piano in the drawing room amid a crush of very well-dressed chattering guests. Xan was treated like a golden god from the moment he arrived, drinks brought, seats found, his every opinion sought. He did once say, 'This is Elvi,' but for the most part, she was studiously ignored, presumably because his habit of having a mistress as a partner at such engagements was well known and she was deemed to be beneath the notice of such wealthy people.

'Who is she?' she heard one woman whisper behind her seat.

'Not his usual type,' another remarked.

'Fabulous hair though. Dyed, of course—'

And Elvi had been horribly tempted to twist

around and disabuse the women with a tart response, but she had resisted the urge, preferring to be ignored while she had to listen to boring financial discussions and Xan kept an unexpectedly possessive arm wrapped round her even while they were sitting down, as if he feared she might bolt for the door.

Perhaps he had ESP, she reflected ruefully, because she was becoming increasingly apprehensive about the end of the evening. She had checked her phone repeatedly, even texting her mother to ask how she was, and if Xan *had* dropped the theft charge the fact hadn't yet been shared with the older woman. How was she supposed to trust him? How was she supposed to know that he had done what he had promised?

'That was a mind-numbing evening,' Xan commented, surprising her as he lounged back in a corner of the limousine. 'I hate it when people fuss over me like that and expect tips for free—'

'The price of success?' Elvi quipped.

As *she* was one of the benefits, Xan savoured, watching her with unashamed hunger. He had used his power to capture her and right at that moment he had not a single regret. She was a natural beauty and blue was definitely *her* colour, lighting up those eyes to brilliance. The wondrous curves were simply the icing on a very tempting cake and tonight she was finally *his*. He had been tempted to cut the party and stay in, had made himself go to convince himself that he was still in control of the need that made him ache with excitement in her radius. Not cool, not cool at all…but now he didn't have to be any longer.

Elvi was not unaware of the way Xan was watching her, could only compare the blaze of those slumberous amber eyes to a panther lazily eying his next meal. Her entire body felt hot and scratchy, her breasts heavy, the space between her thighs tingling and hollow. She knew it was how *he* made her feel and told herself she ought to be grateful for that in the circumstances. Suppose he had not appealed to her in any way? How could she possibly have made such an agreement?

And exactly how was she now supposed to tell him that there was no way she was sharing that bed with him tonight?

Nerves gripped her fast as he accompanied her into the lift and she knew she had to say something. She cleared her throat awkwardly. 'Look… I have something to say—'

'Say it,' Xan urged impatiently, his lean brown hands lifting to come down on her small shoulders and urge her closer even as the lift doors whirred back.

'We…er…*can't*. Not tonight anyway,' she warned him with hot cheeks.

Xan groaned out loud. 'Why didn't you tell me sooner?' he demanded, practically dragging her out of the lift and slotting his own key into the front door of the apartment.

'It was…difficult—'

'Surely you could have rearranged the pills or

something? I would have sent you to the doc-tor, had I known,' Xan growled, pressing her into the apartment and leaning back against the door to close it, his entire brain preoccupied with what he *could* do, what he couldn't and the kind of frustration he had never experienced before engulfing him hard because he was lit-erally *burning* for her.

As Elvi registered what Xan had taken from her declaration, her whole body lit up with em-barrassment because her menstrual cycle was something she had never discussed with any man and the sudden realisation that his access to her was likely to include that kind of personal information appalled her.

'No, you misunderstood me,' she said swiftly. 'It's not *that*—'

'*Diavole*...you're driving me crazy here, *koukla mou*,' Xan growled, curving both his hands to her triangular face to gaze down into her beautiful but evasive eyes. 'What is it?'

But he didn't wait for her response. He fell for

the enticement of those soft pink sultry lips, nibbled sexily along the bottom one, groaned out loud as she gasped into his mouth and bundled her right off her feet to kiss her.

The devastating urgency of that first plunging, ravaging kiss sent an earthquake of burning hunger travelling through Elvi right to the very heart of her. She hadn't thought, hadn't dreamt, hadn't even imagined that she was capable of feeling anything that powerful. But that hunger was like a seductive, sweet-talking infiltrator in her treacherous body, battling every thought, every other instinct and sweeping the floor with her. He blew her away with the sheer raw energy of his mouth on hers, unlocking her defences, connecting with her in a way she had never connected to a man before, making her want him and his body so badly, she felt shell-shocked by the experience, and that very small awareness reawakened her brain again and reminded her of what she had to do…what she had to say…

In a valiant effort, Elvi struggled out of Xan's powerful arms, sliding down the front of his lean, strong body, learning that there was not a shade of doubt that he was as ready for her and that bed as he could ever be, and embarrassment and regret washed over Elvi in a horrible wave.

'I'm so sorry,' she said jerkily, stepping back from Xan, much as if he were contagious. 'But I can't do this yet—'

Xan surfaced faster to study her in disbelief. *'Can't?'* he queried. 'But you *said*—'

'You didn't give me the chance to explain,' Elvi reminded him resolutely, struggling to rise above her chagrined regret over her wanton weakness of body and brain. 'My mother hasn't told me yet that the charge has been dropped and nothing, absolutely *nothing*, is happening between us until I receive that confirmation from her—'

Incredulous as only a young, handsome billionaire could be at meeting with the word no for the first time, Xan raked a slightly shaky hand through his tousled black hair. 'This is you joking...*right*?' he pressed hopefully.

'No, I'm only returning the same favour you gave me,' Elvi assured him without the smallest sense of triumph. 'You said you wouldn't act and drop the theft charge until I moved in here and I had to do that. Now I'm saying that when my *mother* tells me the charge has been dropped, I'm yours but *not* before it—'

A line of dark colour flashed over Xan's exotic cheekbones. 'That's outrageous!' he shot back at her angrily. 'The charge *has* been dropped! I don't break my promises. It's scarcely my fault if the police haven't yet got around to informing her—'

'It's nobody's fault,' Elvi cut in, trying to pour oil on troubled water a little late in the day, she sensed, registering the blaze of frustrated fury smouldering in Xan's amazingly eloquent gaze and the fierce clenched set of his strong jaw. 'But it's the way it is. It's my only safeguard in this arrangement—'

Xan was so outraged, he swung away from her and breathed in deep to muster self-discipline. He wanted to behave like a caveman, gather her up and throw her bodily on the bed and keep her there until she understood who she was dealing with. But he knew he couldn't behave like that, which infuriated him even more. *Her only safeguard*, he reflected in fuming disagreement. Did she really think he was about to break his word when she was standing there with a small fortune in diamonds around her neck and living in his apartment?

Or was it more payback time than safeguard? Payback for the manner in which he had forced her to immediately move in? That made better sense to him, integrating as it did the kind of cunning slyness he hated in her sex but had often experienced. There had been a stepmother who'd tried to seduce him to hit back at his father for his infidelity. There had been mistresses who tried to play games calculated to increase his interest in them, several who told him outrageous lies in an effort to charm more money or jewels out of him. So great was his ire at the suspicion that he had been played by Elvi, he couldn't even bring himself to look at her again or trust himself to speak.

'I'm sorry,' Elvi muttered in the pulsing silence, her hands twisting nervously together in the tense atmosphere. 'I should have told you when I got into the car earlier but I didn't know how to say it. I didn't feel comfortable talking about having sex with you because you're a stranger. I don't suppose you understand but it would be a lot easier if you would allow me to get to know you first.'

Xan's lean brown hands clenched into fists. 'I don't get to know women I have sex with. That's not my style,' he admitted grittily, involuntarily forced out of silence by that naïve little speech of hers. 'Maybe I missed out on asking the one question I *should've* asked in my office last week…are you a prude? Because, to be brutally blunt, you sound like a hell of a prude and that's not going to work for me at all.'

Very pale now, Elvi chewed her lower lip and decided not to respond because silence was safer. Not a prude, a virgin, she almost said, and who could tell how he would react to a surprise like that? Perhaps he was already thinking of letting her go again but would that mean he would reinstate the theft charge? Could he even do that? She had no idea and she was scared and apprehensive, plunged into a relationship she had not the smallest idea how to handle with a man that said stuff that chilled her to the marrowbone.

Xan strode back out of the apartment, still maddeningly taut with an arousal unlike anything he had ever felt before and unnerved by it. *Let her go*, his intelligence told him, cut her free now before it gets even more messy. He wanted her but she could be a disaster waiting to blow up in his face.

He ignored his security team's open surprise

at his almost immediate reappearance, climbed into his limousine and tried to think about walking away fast from Elvi Cartwright because she had taken him to a level of rage he had never felt before and that was disturbing.

Or merely normal? he reasoned, given his sexual frustration. The very last thing he had expected was to end the night with a cold shower. He was beginning to suspect that Elvi might not have even indulged in a one-night stand. Some nauseating romance with a long-term boyfriend struck him as the more likely base of her sexual experience, he decided cynically. She wanted him to get to *know* her? Was she a throwback to the Victorian era? Where did she get a weird idea like that when he had asked her to be his mistress?

Elvi got into the vast bed alone and shivered, still shaken by that confrontation and the kiss that had preceded it. When his mouth had crashed down on hers, she had been overwhelmed by his electrifying sensuality, her physical responses wildly out of her control, but she had pulled back, mustered her strength and finally said what had to be said. And not surprisingly, Xan had been furious because she should have made her position clear at the start of the evening, *not* at the end, she acknowledged guiltily.

Xan Ziakis wasn't accustomed to the word no. He was selfish, arrogant and obsessed with sex. Well, work and sex, she adjusted ruefully. He had expected to take her straight to bed and she had dealt clumsily with those expectations, probably because she *was* the prude he had labelled her. But the concept of sharing her body with someone she didn't even know properly had proved too much for Elvi to cope with on the spot. When she couldn't even imagine taking off her clothes for him, she was in trouble and way outside her comfort zone. Why, oh, why had she ever believed that she could give him what he wanted? That she could simply have sex as if it meant nothing?

And even more inexplicably, why was she just a little disappointed that he hadn't managed to persuade her to change her mind? He hadn't even *tried* to persuade her, had he? Had simply announced that she didn't suit him, rejecting her because she had dared to reject him. Was that it, then? Were they over before they had even begun?

CHAPTER FOUR

SALLY CARTWRIGHT PHONED her daughter mid-morning the next day. 'You'll never guess what's happened,' she burbled in an excited surge. 'The theft charge has been dropped. No explanation, nothing, just the assurance that the complaint has been withdrawn and the police have no further interest.'

'My goodness, that's wonderful news!' Elvi declared brightly, relief rolling through her in a rejuvenating wave of energy. It was done. Xan *had* kept his promise.

Elvi texted him a stiff apology for her lack of confidence, resisting the urge to remind him that he hadn't trusted her either. In truth she didn't know what she was wishing for. That he had ditched her and moved on? In which case she would be moving home again. Or was she stuck with the agreement she had made?

Xan was still in a temper with her when he read the text. He was done with her, *wasn't he*? Last night had been his warning. When you draped a woman in diamonds, threw in a new wardrobe and the use of a very expensive apartment, you expected something in return... *obviously*. It infuriated him that that conviction made *him* feel cheap. It infuriated him that he was tempted to walk out in the middle of his working day and stage a rendezvous with her because he still burned for her. After a sleepless night, the urge to possess Elvi's glorious body was as strong as ever, undaunted by the difficulty of dealing with her unrealistic expectations.

His thought processes were becoming disturbingly insidious and unfamiliar. Every man was entitled to *one* mistake, wasn't he? Why shouldn't he enjoy the mistake he had made and move on afterwards? He texted her that he would be with her that afternoon and endeavoured to get back into the meeting he was in. But he couldn't concentrate, not for wondering what she would be wearing, what she would look like naked, how she would look when he gave her pleasure. In a passion of rare indecision, Xan breathed in deep and slow and wondered what the hell had taken hold of him. He didn't like wanting Elvi as much as he did because such urges smacked of immoderation, indiscipline and chaos, every sin he meticulously avoided in life.

Even so, he stood up in the middle of the meeting and abruptly announced his departure. He would have Elvi one single time and then that would be it. *Once only*, as his mother lamented when she overindulged in chocolate. A treat was one thing, a habit quite another and he did not want a habit like Elvi who took his mind off his work.

Xan texted Elvi.

Coming for lunch.

Was she supposed to cook? Elvi wondered in panic. Or was lunch a euphemism for sex? Was she supposed to greet him in the rather risqué lingerie that had been delivered along with the most massive amount of clothing and accessories earlier that morning? Or was she simply supposed to drape herself somewhere and look inviting? I am *not* a prude, she told her reflection, and then pinched her cheeks because she looked so pale. Maybe she was a prude in comparison to him because *he* seemed to be astonishingly free of inhibitions and self-consciousness. Ironically his ability to be that way made her feel rather envious.

Xan didn't know what he was expecting but he *wasn't* expecting to be greeted by lunch or the shocking disarray of the living area, which ran counter to his every conviction of how an interior should be maintained. Something in the process of being knitted lay abandoned on one sofa and a box of sewing supplies sat on the rug. Books spilled across another seat and the coffee table was littered with random items. There was no organisation, no order. He averted his gaze from it all to focus on her, all anxious blue eyes above pink cheeks, glorious hair framing her face. And he had given her a new wardrobe and what was she wearing? An old denim skirt with a faded top and scuffed cowboy boots, he registered in stupefaction.

'I didn't know whether you'd be hungry or not,' Elvi admitted tightly, striving not to stare at him but, oh, it was difficult not to surrender to base and embarrassing promptings. Xan looked like her every fantasy in one devastating package from the black luxuriance of his hair to the flawless hard lines of his breathtakingly beautiful features, all set within the frame of an exquisitely tailored light grey suit, a white shirt and a crimson silk tie.

'I only have an hour,' Xan imparted, stunned by the food she had prepared because he had never had a mistress who tried to feed him before.

'Oh...'

'I'm only hungry for you,' Xan intoned huskily while wondering if he should draw up a list of rules to urge her in the right direction—tidy up, don't feed me, wear the clothes I give you—and then his attention locked onto the voluptuous pink lower lip she was chewing on and the throb at his groin overpowered every other thought and he simply reached for her.

He snatched her up into his arms and kissed her breathless and a sort of giddy, unfamiliar delight pierced Elvi, because Xan Ziakis could wreak havoc on her body with one extraordinary kiss. So, when the kisses piled up, she got lost in them, which in its own way was a relief because it stopped her overthinking stuff and held the nerves at bay. Her arms snaked round his neck as he carried her out of the kitchen and her momentary panic had subsided to be replaced by a helpless sense of anticipation. She was finally coming to terms with the truth that she wanted him too and that there was nothing one-sided about their chemistry.

Abandoned clothing festooned the single chair in the bedroom. Xan ignored the display, for once too caught up in the wonder of Elvi's response to notice. She tasted like strawberries and the soft damp welcome of her mouth inflamed him. He wanted that wondrous mouth of hers everywhere on him. In fact colourful images were tumbling through Xan's head and making control a rare challenge. *One time only,* he reminded himself doggedly, like a man trying to bargain with the devil, as he settled her down on the bed.

'I need a shower,' Xan confided, yanking loose his tie beneath her arrested gaze. 'Join me—'

The prospect of getting naked with him in a shower was a step too far too fast for Elvi and she gave him a tense smile. 'I'll just wait here.'

Xan was used to women who did exactly what he wanted when he wanted and he was disconcerted afresh by her reluctance. The instant one of the bathroom doors closed on him, Elvi leapt off the bed to buzz the blinds shut and undress at frantic speed. She had already had two showers that morning, one when she got up, the second after he texted her. She climbed back into the bed naked, every skin cell on high alert for his reappearance.

She wished she weren't so shy. Prudish, he had called it, but she was painfully aware that what was amiss with her was inexperience and a lack of confidence in her own body. At school the majority of her peers had been skinny and leggy and that had made her feel chunky and unfashionable, for the trendy clothing that had flattered their slimmer curves had done nothing for her very different shape. Nor could she escape the demeaning suspicion that the minute Xan saw her naked, he would realise that she wasn't quite the bombshell he had hoped.

But then what did any of that matter? she censured herself in exasperation. They had an agreement, not a relationship based on caring or commitment. It was only sex and it only seemed more of a challenge to her because sex was new to her. She had to assume that a womaniser would know what he was doing in the bedroom and by this evening she would probably be wondering what all the fuss was about. Her expectations were low. She might find Xan irresistibly attractive but the prospect of getting hot, sweaty and naked with a stranger still intimidated her.

The bathroom door opened and Xan emerged, towelling his hair dry; a naked bronzed muscular vision of masculinity in her shaken appraisal. No, Xan was definitely *not* shy. He seemed a little surprised by the dimness of the room and frowned as he crawled up lithely from the bottom of the bed, evidently equally surprised to find her waiting there for him. He reached up to stab the lights on.

'I like it dim—'

'I don't.' A slanting grin tilted Xan's wide sensual mouth. 'I lay awake half the night thinking about this moment—'

'Truthfully?' Elvi framed unevenly.

'You really do it for me,' Xan growled, yanking back the sheet she was cringing below. '*Thee mou*...what glorious breasts!'

Elvi just shut her eyes tight and lay there barely breathing, for an instant barely crediting that only a few minutes earlier she had believed she wanted him as much as he wanted her. And then he hauled her under him and crushed her ripe mouth under his and once again everything changed so fast that her head spun dizzily. She wondered what magic there was to his mouth on hers that made her crave more, her fingers skimming up his cheekbones into his silky cropped hair and holding him to her.

A kiss is only a kiss, she thought abstractedly, but it wasn't with Xan, it was fireworks and wild passion and the delving, curling intimacy of his tongue flicking inside her mouth, setting off a chain reaction that arrowed through her body with a piercing, burning sweetness that made her hips rise helplessly off the mattress.

He touched her breasts and she ached and quivered, the swollen, straining buds of her nipples shockingly responsive to the tug of his fingers and then the warm wet torment of his mouth, his tongue, his teeth…and her back arched, a sliding liquidity and heat rising in her pelvis because every touch felt as amazing as the hot, hard, muscular weight of him pinning her to the bed. He shifted back a little, muttering something in Greek, pausing to kiss her again with a hungry ferocity that made her heart beat stronger and faster than ever, excitement building as he stroked her thigh, parted her legs, finally touching her where she craved being touched. And at that point, everything became increasingly hazy for Elvi because she was out of control and pushed to a fever pitch by the intense sensitivity of her own body. Skilled fingers rubbed, delicately explored the sleek, silky depths of her, little tremors pulling at her, little sounds wrenched from her parted lips, the excitement blazing over her and soaring through her like leaping flames.

Burning all over, she writhed, yearning for more but too out of her mind to even recognise what more entailed. Xan's wide sensual mouth crashed down on hers again and it was as if she had stuck a finger in an electric socket because for an instant, with her heart hammering and her breath clawing for escape from her constricted lungs, that spellbinding kiss enthralled her. And then he slid over her, lifting her thighs, pinning them back. Somehow the weight of him and that intimate contact were what her body craved.

Xan plunged into her heated core with passionate force. Elvi jerked and twisted her head away at the fierce jolt of pain, no longer flying in a delicious play world of the physical, suddenly brought back down to earth with a crash. Tears stung her eyes and she closed them tight, sealing herself off in an instinctive need for privacy, recognising that what she had mindlessly craved felt more like a punishment than a pleasure. Mercifully the pain faded as fast as it had come and her tension disappeared with it. Different sensations began to coalesce within her as he changed his angle, tilted her up and an almost forgotten jab of excitement tightened like a band low in her belly.

And then he kissed her again, claiming her reddened lips with hungry need, and she reconnected with him, compelled by the convulsive little quivers travelling through her pelvis and the almost mystical push of elation beginning to grip her every nerve. Never had she been more aware of anything than the sleek, hard invasion of his body into hers, stretching her, rousing her with his dynamic drive. The peak of pleasure took her by surprise, throwing her up in a gasping breathless wave to the heights and then letting her fall, slowly, gently while the ripples of delight were still convulsing her.

Xan pulled back, convinced he had just enjoyed the best sex of his life and shocked by the wildness of it and the alarming awareness that he had lost control. And then *two* unexpected events drove all such ruminations from mind. He was about to head for the bathroom to dispose of the condom when he suddenly registered that he hadn't *used* one, a reckless omission that nothing could excuse and which froze him in his tracks. In that interim instant of inaction and disbelief he noticed the blood on the sheet.

'You're bleeding,' he noted jerkily. 'Did I hurt you?'

Raw mortification assailed Elvi and she squirmed away from him, yanking the top sheet over the embarrassing proof of her inexperience. 'No, it was my first time,' she muttered tightly, her face suffusing with chagrined heat.

CHAPTER FIVE

XAN COMPUTED THAT admission and he was so shocked by the revelation, he literally felt sick. His lethally accurate brain threw up the entirety of his dealings with Elvi Cartwright and shame engulfed him for the first time in his life because such a scenario, a sordid scenario in which he demanded sex from an innocent girl, appalled him. It had not once crossed his mind that at her age she could be literally *untouched*. No, not these days, when he was forever reading about young women treating sex as casually as young men and when he himself was offered sex as carelessly as a handshake at first meetings. He utterly recoiled from the image of himself as a violator of virgins. If he had known, he would have kept his distance, would never *ever* have suggested…

'Why the *hell* didn't you tell me that?' Xan demanded rawly, sliding off the bed in one powerful movement. 'Naturally I assumed that you had sexual experience—'

Shot from the heights of her first real orgasm to the depths of embarrassment and then held trapped there by the unexpectedly angry reaction of her first lover, Elvi wrapped herself in the sheet and raised her knees to her chin, linking her arms round her trembling legs. 'But why would you assume that?' she asked shakily.

Xan raked an unsteady hand through his tousled black hair. 'Because that's the norm at your age. If I'd known you were a virgin, I would *never* have touched you and I would *never* have offered you the arrangement that I did!' he shot at her furiously.

Elvi was perplexed because Xan had not impressed her as a man with sincere moral principles and she shrugged a rounded shoulder in dismissal of that statement. 'It's a little late now for regrets,' she pointed out. 'I did warn you that I wasn't really suitable for what you had in mind but you weren't interested in hearing it.'

Xan was never interested in hearing anything that conflicted with his own needs and wants and he didn't require a stinging reminder from her that he had made an inexcusable mistake. Dark colour laced his high cheekbones and, with gritted teeth, he spun and strode towards the bathroom, only to freeze again and turn lithely back to her.

'Are you on the pill?'

Elvi shook her head. 'Why would I have been?'

'On any form of contraception?' Xan persisted tautly.

'No. I was planning to sort something out this week but the very tight timetable you imposed on me prevented me from doing anything in advance,' she said shortly.

'You should've told me you were a virgin!' Xan lashed back at her with unconcealed censure.

'Why?' Elvi countered. 'It was none of your business!'

'It became *my* business when you were planning to have a sexual relationship with me,' Xan contradicted with controlled savagery.

'As you well know, you were the one who planned to have a sexual relationship with me and I had to move in here barely twelve hours after agreeing, so my planning *anything* didn't come into it!'

Xan shuddered at the burn of being force-fed the truth on an unappetising plate. He and no one else had brought about this disaster. His arrogance, his ego had resulted in this mess and it was a lesson he had never expected to receive because for too many years he had been invincible, his every move lauded, his every deal a phenomenal success. It seemed he was not the man he had been raised to become, not the person he had believed himself to be. It was a pivotal moment for him, glancing round the spacious room where he had spent so many hours with forgettable women and inwardly cringing at how he had foolishly believed he had it made with that set-up, because that detached conveyor-belt system had now gone badly wrong for him. And he *still* didn't know how to fix it…

Elvi's clasped hands round her knees tightened, her knuckles showing white below her skin. She was a little ball of rigid tension in recognition of his. Presumably he was disappointed. That was why he was angry. Angry not with her, she sensed, but with himself for a poor choice of playmate.

'I'm not what you expected,' she said for him.

Xan swallowed hard. 'No,' he conceded, wondering how the hell he was supposed to make amends. 'You surprised me. Very few people manage to do that.'

Let her go, Xan reasoned. It was the obvious answer to fixing what was wrong but he looked at her, all wrapped round herself as if she was trying to make herself small, and his chest tightened and he hauled in a long rasping breath, his broad chest expanding. He didn't want the obvious answer and he was *still* a selfish bastard, he acknowledged, because he still wanted her. Even when he could see the shininess of tears in her bright blue eyes. What did that say about him? That he was capable of wanting an unwilling woman? No way would he touch her again without an invitation from *her*, he told himself squarely, rationalising an irrational decision. He would make amends. He didn't know how but in some mysterious way he would manage that feat. He was very clever. He would work it out eventually.

'I think I'll eat that lunch you were kind enough to make me,' Xan said abruptly.

Astonishment flashed through Elvi and her lashes lowered on her anxious eyes. He was still imprinted on her eyelids, a spectacular bronzed man naked as a jaybird, standing there like a stone statue, his discomfiture obvious to her. What was the matter with him? The soft sounds of him dressing, the click of cuff links snapping closed, the sound of a zip penetrated her shell of silence. She had had sex for the very first time and *he* had disappointed *her* because he had denied the intimacy of the experience, pulling away as soon as he was done, and none of the pleasure he had given her had made up for that distance and reserve.

'What are you thinking about?' Xan prompted, more uncomfortable than he had ever been in his entire life with a woman.

'I'm lonely,' Elvi muttered truthfully. 'I'm used to having my family around—'

'I'm here,' Xan reminded her.

'But you're not cuddly,' Elvi told him apologetically.

Xan grimaced. 'No. Is that what you like?'

'It's not the kind of physical you're used to,' Elvi guessed wryly, wondering how she had given herself to such a man, wondering how she could look into those hard, dark but stunning eyes and want to give herself again, want to make him smile for once and hear him laugh.

'I hug my mother,' he declared in his own defence.

'Even you have to have one weakness,' Elvi quipped.

'Lunch,' Xan reminded her. 'Why don't you join me?'

Wrapping the sheet round herself with innate modesty, Elvi headed into the other bathroom and went for a very quick shower. In some ways, she was in shock. His possession had hurt more than she had been prepared for and then had come the pleasure that had also been more than she had expected. For the first time, she understood why Xan Ziakis was so hooked on sex. He was good at it too, she conceded ruefully, because he had turned a bad start into something truly amazing and then trashed that by moving away from her afterwards, as if, once he got his satisfaction, he was keen to forget who had given it to him. It had made her feel used, unappreciated. She should have anticipated that. Sex was only sex for him. He didn't look to receive anything beyond that fleeting physical thrill.

He was still in the bedroom, his back turned to

her when she emerged breathless from hurrying out of the fancy dressing room. She had worn something new from what Sylvia had described as a basic 'capsule' wardrobe, but which covered more garments than she had ever owned in her entire life at one and the same time. And apparently, even more clothes tailored to her precise requirements would eventually arrive. The skirt she had chosen was short and flirty, the top thin silk, the sandals high-heeled. Did she look like a proper mistress now? she wondered unhappily. Would he actually look at her again? For some reason, he seemed to be avoiding looking. The strangeness of his behaviour was starting to wear on her. She hated the knowledge that she didn't know what was going on inside his head. But why did she even *want* to know? That was a question she couldn't answer.

'Lunch,' she murmured, thankful she had only made a salad and not something that would have spoiled.

Xan swung round, immediately noticing the

clothing, tensing because it gave her a much more sophisticated look than her own clothing did, reminding him that right from the start he had tried to make her into something she wasn't, ignoring the signs that she was different, an individual, trying to make her over into the kind of sleek, faceless sex object he was comfortable with. That suspicion unnerved him because he wasn't accustomed to examining his own motives or to seeing how his stubborn determination to treat all his mistresses the same had ensured that he flatly refused to acknowledge that Elvi might be unique.

Xan was so tall, so dark he snarled up the breath in Elvi's dry throat. A jolt of wanton response curled warm and low in her pelvis, which amused her because had he tried to touch her again she probably would have screamed because she was sore, way too sore to desire further intimacy.

In a determined movement, she left the bedroom and went into the kitchen to serve the chicken salad. While she would have been happy to eat at the kitchen table, she reckoned Xan would baulk and she carried the plates out to the more formal dining area. He sank down into a chair within seconds of her taking a seat. For an instant, she allowed herself to look at him. The guy was insanely hot from those killer cheekbones to the shadow of stubble accentuating the fullness of his sensual lips. Heat mushroomed up inside her and she immediately dropped her head to eat.

Xan glanced around himself, disliking the familiarity of the room and the recollections of how he had spent his time there. He would sell the place, would never return to it, he decided at lightning speed. He couldn't wait to remove Elvi from surroundings which only reminded him of what he would prefer to forget. The answer of what to do next came to him and his cautious streak fired up. He would be breaking a habit, decimating his usual routine, but slavishly following that routine and indulging those habits had subjected him to several far from commendable discoveries about his own nature.

'Tomorrow, I am leaving early in the morning for Greece,' he murmured flatly. 'There is a wedding in my family and I must attend. I would like you to accompany me.'

Elvi was sharply disconcerted and a piece of chicken almost went down the wrong way because her throat tightened like all the rest of her in surprise. *'Me?'* she queried uncertainly.

'You see anyone else sitting here?' Xan said drily.

Elvi flushed and went back to eating.

'You have a passport?' he checked.

Elvi nodded. Her mother had spent her last bonus on equipping the three of them with passports. They had had a dream of travelling abroad for a few days, something cut price and last-minute and cheap. Of course, that prospect had died with Sally's dismissal, along with everything else. Like life as she *had* known it, Elvi conceded ruefully. Only a couple of days had passed since she had worked in the craft shop, going home each evening to her family. Xan had taken *everything*, she thought unhappily.

Xan had never been with such a quiet woman and it unsettled him. He had expected a modest amount of enthusiasm to greet the kind of invitation he had never given a woman before. Of course, she probably didn't appreciate that reality. But she had mentioned *wanting* to get to know him, hadn't she? What better opportunity could he offer her? It crossed his mind that possibly she no longer wanted to get to know him better, but he brushed off the suspicion with all the instinctive disdain of a man accustomed to being the number one, highly desirable target of every young woman in his radius.

'I'll send a car to pick you up at nine this evening,' Xan announced, rising lithely upright. 'It will be more convenient if you spend the night before we travel at my apartment.'

Elvi rose to follow him to the door, although she didn't know why she was offering him that courtesy when he had his own key to the apartment. He was already on his mobile phone, uttering what sounded like instructions to someone in another language. Greek? She had no idea, having only studied French at school.

For a split second, Xan hovered on the threshold and looked back at her, feeling weirdly uneasy about abandoning her when it was obvious that she was missing her family so much. Her glow wasn't back, he noted, thinking grimly that he had successfully killed that. An air of nervous uncertainty lay in her small restive movements. He hadn't discussed the pregnancy risk. It wasn't the moment, he told himself squarely, because she hadn't noticed that contraceptive mishap. Why worry her about something so unlikely? What were the chances after one encounter? Slim, to none, he reasoned, and he offered up his first inner prayer since childhood in support of that hope. Wasn't he already feeling guilty enough? Surely that ultimate axe would not also fall on him?

Elvi met Xan's dazzling amber eyes and it was as though a mental ping of recognition sounded somewhere deep within her own brain. He was upset about something. She didn't know how she knew that but somehow she did, belatedly recognising that nobody could be quite as detached from the rest of humanity as he liked to appear. And such beautiful eyes he had, lushly enclosed between black velvet lashes, such an amazing colour and surprisingly eloquent. Her body reacted with shocking intensity, her breasts tightening while a sensation of awareness purred between her thighs.

'H-how long will we be in Greece?' she asked abruptly, battling that awareness with fierce discomfiture.

'Five days,' Xan said in a roughened undertone, wondering how the hell he was going to keep his hands off her when she could turn him on so fast she made him feel like an animal.

Not that that was so very far from the truth concerning their single encounter, Xan reminded himself with gritted teeth as he strode into the lift, refusing to allow himself to linger, thoroughly distrusting, indeed loathing, the powerful sexual urges pulling at him. He had already fallen on Elvi once with all the refinement of a sex-starved teenager, so out of himself that he had forgotten protection and had failed to note that he had hurt her. Scarcely a stellar show of sophistication or skill. No way was he about to repeat that idiocy.

Determined to get every change made instantly, Xan contacted the concierge company to organise the removal of Elvi's possessions from the apartment and the sale of it. He was still issuing instructions when he climbed into the limousine and was absently aware of Dmitri's frowning face. What the hell was up with his head of security? Dmitri Pallas had been with Xan for years. A former inspector in the Greek police force, he was very efficient in his field. But of recent, crucially the placing of

Elvi's letter in the cause of Sally Cartwright, Dmitri's behaviour had been strange.

Already feeling unusually hassled, Xan shelved the acknowledgement as something else to deal with at a more opportune time. Maybe Dmitri had family problems or something. Maybe he knew more about that theft business than he had been willing to share. Whatever, Xan was in no mood to delve into anything that could verge on the personal. It was a direction he never went in with his staff because he valued his own privacy too highly. And the day when he blew his own cherished privacy sky-high was not a day when he felt prompted to break down barriers with others.

A woman in his apartment, even if it was only for *one* night, was a major departure from the norm for him. Should he have put her in a hotel? No, that would've been shabby, he decided, and his behaviour had been shabby enough for one day, hadn't it?

While Xan was contemplating the challenge

of sharing his space for even one night, Elvi was on the way home for a visit, unable to sit alone in the empty apartment even though she knew she would either have to lie or evade the truth as the price of that family visit. The knowledge made her sad but the dropping of the theft charge was, in her opinion, a worthwhile return, regardless of the dishonesty it had involved her in.

She was startled when she got home to find her mother actually turning out cupboards and packing the contents into boxes.

'What on earth are you doing?' she asked her mother from the kitchen doorway.

Sally smiled up at her daughter from her position on her knees on the floor.

'We're moving to Oxford in a few days…'

Elvi's brow furrowed, her eyes uncomprehending. 'I don't understand—'

Sally picked herself up. 'I'll make us a cup of tea and explain,' she said, visibly in a far better state of mind than she had been the last time

Elvi actually saw her, with something of her usual bustling energy back in her step and voice.

'Dmitri Pallas…the head of Mr Ziakis's security team…is a good friend of mine,' Sally advanced with a slight deepening of colour. 'He's come to our rescue…'

Her brow furrowing, Elvi sank down at the table while her mother brewed the tea. 'You've never mentioned him before,' she pointed out uncomfortably.

'Didn't see the need because I used to see him every day at work,' Sally Cartwright told her wryly. 'And no, there's no romance there, nothing but friendship, and I don't know if there ever could be but I do like him very much.'

'Nothing wrong with that,' Elvi said gently, disconcerted by her mother's fluctuating colour and embarrassment. No romance, yeah, as if she was going to believe that with *that* look on the older woman's face! She thought of the man whom she had met so briefly, the warm concern she had seen in his eyes over that letter. She thought of Sally's lost years and of how in all the time since she'd lost her husband her mother had had not a single man in her life… and then she thought of how wonderful it would be if her parent could finally have something nice in her life, something for her rather than the children she adored.

'Well, Dmitri has a little house in Oxford because he has family living in the area,' Sally proffered. 'He knows how we're fixed financially and, now that I've lost my job…well, he's found me another one there with a connection of his. Waitressing, a step up from cleaning, I think—'

'Yes,' Elvi agreed.

'We're to stay in Dmitri's house initially and then, when we get on our feet again, we can move on to somewhere of our own. He doesn't live there…*ever*,' Sally added stiltedly. 'Mr Ziakis travels abroad a lot and Dmitri travels with him. Dmitri buys property as an investment for when he retires.'

'You'll be in Oxford for the beginning of Daniel's classes,' Elvi remarked approvingly.

'Yes…' Sally smiled suddenly, all her natural warmth on display as she hugged her daughter's shoulders where she sat. 'Isn't it amazing how life can just suddenly take a turn for the better?'

'Amazing,' Elvi agreed.

'My only concern is that I'm going to see less of you.' Sally sighed.

'Can't have everything,' Elvi quipped. 'And I can still visit.'

'Can I ask you just *one* question?' Sally prompted anxiously. 'Why can't we meet this boyfriend of yours?'

Elvi tried and failed to fit Xan Ziakis into the boyfriend category and reddened. 'It's…er…too soon,' she mumbled uncomfortably.

'So, it *has* been one of those "love at first sight" efforts, then,' Sally assumed, seeming to relax at that idea. 'He hasn't been around long—'

'And it could end as quickly as it started,' Elvi dared to add.

Sally grimaced as she made the tea. 'I won't wish *that* on you...but it would mean you could move to Oxford and join us.'

'Probably,' Elvi allowed, cupping her hands round the warm mug, her turmoil over Xan soothed by her mother's restored spirits.

And why did she even feel that she was in turmoil over him? she questioned with self-loathing. They had had sex and that was all. There was nothing more to them. They were not a couple in a relationship. And if she was learning things she would sooner not have known, well, that was part of growing up, she told herself impatiently. The first lesson had been that she could enjoy intimacy without the finer feelings getting involved, and she hadn't been proud of that until Xan's detachment in the aftermath had wounded her, teaching her that while she might *tell* herself that she expected nothing more, she was still somehow programmed to *want* more from the man than he was ever likely to give her.

Only a couple of minutes before nine, Elvi returned to the apartment and was perplexed to find it stripped of everything she owned. Where was her stuff? It meant she couldn't change out of the jeans she had gone home in, even had she wanted to.

And why would she want to? she asked herself irritably. Pleasing Xan by wearing the clothes he had bought for her shouldn't be on her to-do list. In fact the sooner he got tired of her, she told herself, the better it would be for both of them. A trip to Greece in his company wasn't likely to change anything between them and they had nothing whatsoever in common beyond the fact that they had both been born human.

CHAPTER SIX

SHORTLY AFTER NINE, Elvi was wafted away from the apartment to Xan's penthouse.

There was nothing comfortable about that experience, primarily because Xan *wasn't* at the penthouse to greet her. Dmitri informed her with positive cheerfulness that his employer was attending a bankers' dinner at a private club, and left her to wander alone around the most amazing living space Elvi had ever seen.

It astonished her that here was only *one* massive bedroom, because her mother had never mentioned that fact, or that there was a gym. Of course, he had to make the effort to keep fit when he was in a desk job, she reasoned while a flood of spontaneous images of Xan's lean, muscular physique filled her memory to overflowing. Her face burned up and she registered that she had changed, he had changed her, whether she liked it or not.

The living area was all space and contemporary furniture, the bedroom simply empty by comparison until she peeked into the closets her mother had mentioned and discovered the marvels of Xan's need to classify everything into a category, and it made her wonder *why* he was that way. Her clothing was also to be discovered in a closet, but it hadn't been colour-coded. There was only one en-suite bathroom, and it contained a magnificent sunken bath that called to Elvi much like a siren's song after the day she had endured. Evidently Xan enjoyed a puritanical bathing experience because there were no perfumed lotions and nothing that made bubbles, but she sank into the warm depths of the water regardless, only then appreciating how very tired she was.

All that fretting about her first experience of sex had taken it out of her, not to mention the awkward aftermath when Xan had treated her much like a stranger to whom he had to be polite, she reflected wearily. In a minute she would get out of the bath and climb into the only bed available.

Taking his security team by surprise, Xan left the official dinner early. It felt very odd to him to picture someone waiting for him at the penthouse and he suppressed the observation, exasperated by the unusual thoughts interfering with his normally disciplined state of mind. He stalked into his bedroom, spotted a little pile of clothes on the floor and frowned. Well, she was here but *where*?

He walked round the entire apartment before deciding that she had to be in the bathroom and only then noticed that the door was slightly ajar. He pushed it quietly wide and saw her fast asleep in his bath and sunk low enough in the water for it to be dangerous. Jawline clenching, he reached for a large towel before reaching for her. She wakened, startled and apparently stricken to find herself in his arms, bright blue eyes filled with alarm. 'What? Where?' she framed in dismay.

'You fell asleep,' he told her as her torrent of hair dripped everywhere as if she were a mermaid dragged suddenly from the sea.

'What are you doing with me?'

'I was putting you in bed—'

'But I can't go to bed with *wet* hair!' she gasped.

Mouth compressing, Xan set her down again. 'Just wrap it in a towel and go to bed,' he urged.

'Have you any idea what it would look like in the morning if I did that?' Elvi exclaimed in receipt of that ill-advised male suggestion.

'Does it matter?' Xan traded from the doorway.

Elvi huffed and knotted the overly large towel round her ribcage to prevent it from falling and exposing her even more. Having found her naked in the bath, he had already seen it all anyway, she reminded herself ruefully. She dug into her toiletries bag for a comb and met his brilliant dark eyes in the mirror. 'I'll dry it,' she muttered unevenly, disconcerted by the reality that he was still standing there.

'Don't fall asleep in the bath again. It's dangerous—'

'I'm not elderly or infirm. First taste of water I got would've wakened me!' Elvi told him with spirit. 'Tell me, do you always imagine the worst possible consequences from every event?'

'Pretty much.' Xan was studying her, noting the porcelain fairness of her skin below the lights, remembering how soft she had felt under him, the little sounds she had made, the dreamy look on her face when she climaxed. Hunger throbbed through him like a powerful drug, seriously disturbing him.

'Thought so,' Elvi confided cheerfully, finished combing and reaching for the dryer on the wall.

'There's something we have to discuss,' Xan told her tautly then.

'And what's that?' Elvi pressed, her hand falling back from the dryer.

'I failed to use a condom with you today—'

'What?' Elvi gasped in disbelief as she twisted around to look directly at him, heavy wet strands of hair snaking across her bare shoulders. 'You mean…we had unprotected *sex*?'

Lean, strong features set hard, Xan jerked his chin in confirmation.

'Are you crazy?' Elvi framed in horror. 'Why didn't you—?'

'I lost control… I forgot. I made a mistake. It's that simple,' Xan interposed in a tone of curt finality. 'Obviously I'm furious with myself, but I have regular health checks and there is no danger of—'

'But what if you've got me pregnant?' Elvi interrupted, her anxiety on that score overpowering her usual need to avoid any kind of intimate discussion.

'I think there is very little danger of that after *one* sexual encounter,' Xan informed her with impressive confidence, and some of her tension drained away because his unwavering assurance did have a soothing effect on her. 'It's most unlikely. I apologise, though, for causing the scare.'

'No, I should've thought about the risk too,' Elvi muttered uncomfortably, striving to be reasonable. 'I should've checked but I didn't even think about that…er…aspect.'

In the bedroom, Xan undressed for a shower, automatically putting everything in its designated space. Busy drying her mane of hair, Elvi didn't appear to notice him entering or leaving the shower and he slid into bed first, achingly aroused and knowing there was no possibility of relief. With a groan he turned over and punched a pillow, catching sight of her rustling through a drawer, emptying half of it in pursuit of what she wanted and then piling what remained back in and actually *forcing* the drawer closed on it. He tried to imagine living with that kind of disorder and almost shuddered, while covertly watching below his cloaking lashes as she crossed the room clad in the pyjamas from hell, which covered her from head and toe. She switched out the light on the far side of the bed and clambered in.

The bedding smelt vaguely of Xan, Elvi conceded sleepily, and it was an oddly comforting scent. She refused to lie awake fretting about the possibility of an unplanned pregnancy, dimly deciding that Xan probably knew the odds better than her. If it happened, that would be time enough to worry, she told herself. There was no advantage to agonising in advance, and in any case she would have the confirmation one way or another within a very short time.

He had given her something more to think about than the reality that she was sharing a bed with a man for the first time ever overnight, while she hoped he had got the message via the pyjamas that she was unavailable for anything more entertaining than sleep. Of course she knew there were other things that could be done that did not entail the final act that had left her body aching, but she was impossibly tired from all the stress of recent days.

'Night, Xan,' she mumbled, as if he were her roommate, and minutes later she was sound asleep.

Xan lay awake marvelling at her seeming indifference to his presence. Random thoughts bombarded him like shrapnel. Was it an act aimed at challenging him? He really didn't think so because there was nothing inviting or even slightly tantalising about those pyjamas. Obviously, she didn't like her new wardrobe and he would have to try harder in that department. He had never actually spent the whole night with a woman before but did Elvi know that? Did she even *care*?

And what had happened to *wanting* to get to know him? D for effort, Elvi, he mused, hugely irritated.

Elvi slept like a log and woke up in a surprisingly good mood. After all, yesterday she had crossed the sex bridge and now that apprehension was overcome, she reminded herself with determination. In addition, her mother and her brother were safe from prosecution and would soon be starting a new chapter in Oxford. Buoyant at how the worst of her fears had been vanquished, she bestowed a faint smile on Xan as he strolled out of the bathroom, immaculately dressed in his usual formal suit and looking spectacular as usual.

'I haven't even packed,' she exclaimed in sudden dismay.

It was the very first time she had smiled at him. Xan immediately forgave her for sleeping like the dead in his bed. 'It's very warm in Greece,' he pointed out. 'You'll need different clothing and I've taken care of it—'

'Oh, not *more* clothes!' Elvi complained in dismay, her nose wrinkling. 'I don't need anything more. Honestly, I can make do fine with what I've already got—'

'I will not be seen in public with a woman

who is making do,' Xan declared with perceptible distaste.

'Of course, if you're going to be snobbish about it—'

'I'm not snobbish,' Xan asserted in a roughened undertone. 'But I do not wish you to be embarrassed by being inappropriately dressed.'

Elvi got out of bed, as inappropriately dressed as any woman Xan had ever seen and she exhibited zero embarrassment over that reality. The pyjamas were downright ugly, baggy and shapeless on her small form as she breezed past him into the bathroom. Having Elvi for the night hadn't proved much different from having one of his five-year-old nieces sleeping over. It was clean and innocent, not something that had much appeal for him. Belatedly he reminded himself that her stay and the trip were supposed to be all about her and *not* about him. He needed to ease his conscience and rise above the guilt and regret she had roused in him the day before. But there was no pressure on him to *enjoy* the process…

Having established that it was barely six in the morning—no, Xan had not been joking about that early start—Elvi dressed in haste and joined him for breakfast in the elegant dining room. She was unsettled by the realisation that she was excited about travelling abroad for the very first time. Xan, however, seemed rather downbeat and prone to wincing when she spoke, necessarily dragging his attention from the newspaper he was reading. 'Aren't you pleased that you're going to see your family today?' she pressed.

His high cheekbones pulled taut below his stunning amber eyes, his beautifully moulded mouth compressing. 'I'm not particularly close to my siblings.'

'But you're the eldest,' she said in surprise, adding a third spoon of sugar to her coffee beneath Xan's frowning gaze. 'Don't they turn to you for advice? I know Daniel does with me—'

'They do,' Xan confirmed. 'I look after them.

That's my duty but that doesn't mean they're my best friends. I help them with problems—'

'How many siblings do you have?'

'Six,' Xan said succinctly. 'Four half-sisters, two half-brothers.'

'So…' Elvi rested inquisitive eyes on his lean, darkly handsome visage, momentarily reminding him of a baby bird seeking a titbit '…that means either your mother *or* your father had more than one marriage—'

'My father was a five times loser at the altar,' Xan supplied drily. 'Two models and two beauty queens followed my mother and all four wives were greedy to feather their own nests.'

'Oh…' Elvi said nothing more, understanding a little more about his background than she had previously because a multi-married father, a possibly betrayed mother and a bunch of half-siblings implied a fairly dysfunctional family history, compared with her own. But she was reluctantly impressed by Xan's assurance that he looked after his younger siblings, even though he didn't consider himself close to them. 'So, whose wedding are we attending?'

'Delphina, the youngest one. She's twenty. At an age when she ought to be out forging a career and a lively social life, she's tying herself down,' Xan declared with cynical disapproval. 'She and Takis will be in the divorce court within five years.'

Elvi winced. 'If they truly love each other they'll make it through,' she argued.

Xan rolled his eyes, unimpressed, and rustled his newspaper before dropping his head to give the printed word his full attention again. A shard of sunlight shone across the glossy blue-black strands of his hair, which he wore longer on top, shorn short at the sides. His wickedly long black lashes shielded his gaze from her, drawing her eyes down the straight blade of his nose to the faint dark shadow of stubble that shaded his golden skin even soon after shaving. Blinking in confusion, Elvi looked away, questioning her fascination, denying the licking little curl of heat uncoiling between her thighs, pressing them together to stop that betrayal in its tracks.

She had to be his mistress but that didn't mean she had to like it or blindly accept that she was attracted to him. She wasn't going to play that game to his rules, wasn't going to let sex seduce her into being disloyal to her own ideals. She didn't want sex *without* feelings involved and wasn't about to let her body mislead her. She was stronger than that…wasn't she? If she let herself sink without trace into that sexual chemistry, it would only encourage him to hang on to her longer. And she didn't want that, of course she didn't, she told herself firmly.

As Elvi drifted away from the table with all the precise direction of a dandelion seed blowing in the breeze, Xan watched her pause to look out of the window, almost trip over a chair and only then head towards the door. She lived inside her head more than she lived in the real world, he thought impatiently. Her nature was utterly alien to his and he couldn't understand why he had the most ridiculous urge to smooth her passage through every obstacle.

Returning to the bedroom, intending to make a start on that packing to be ready for their departure in an hour's time, Elvi was perplexed to find Sylvia already there with suitcases and an assistant.

'Tell me what you want to bring with you to Greece,' Sylvia urged helpfully, as if it was no big deal to be standing in someone else's bedroom working before seven in the morning.

Being rushed through the VIP channel at the airport only heightened Elvi's sense of anticipation, no matter how hard she tried to suppress it, and, stepping onto Xan's sleek private jet, she was unable to silence a small gasp of awe at the space in the cabin furnished with ivory leather seating and the kind of luxuries that even she, who had never flown before, knew were extravagances available only to the very wealthy. The svelte stewardess offered her an array of different coffees, a library of films, all the latest glossy magazines and even the option of a lie-down in the stateroom.

'Take a seat,' Xan instructed her tersely, wondering why she was still hovering in the middle of the aisle.

'It's my first flight,' she whispered, not wanting any of the smartly uniformed cabin crew around them to hear. 'I can't help staring—'

Xan closed a hand over hers and settled her down in the seat opposite his. 'Life's just full of firsts for you right now.'

Elvi dealt him a stonily unamused glance and lifted her chin.

'I'm not making fun of you… I'm *not*,' Xan insisted, working hard not to laugh at that look she had given him, which had washed off him like a feather trying to beat up a rock. 'But why haven't you flown before? For most people it's like catching a bus these days.'

'You really don't have a clue what my life has been like.'

'Then educate me.'

'You'd be bored,' Elvi told him repressively, having caught the gleam of amusement in his gaze at her earlier naïve admission.

His expectant silence nagged at her. 'Obviously we never had the money to go on holidays,' she admitted unwillingly.

'Then why have a passport?'

'Equally obviously people still like to live in hope.'

'Even with an alcoholic parent?'

'Sally went through a very tough time after my father died but she still adopted me,' Elvi proclaimed defensively.

'Adopted?' Xan shot her a startled glance. 'You were adopted?'

Elvi sighed. 'My mother was my father's first wife but she died when I was a baby. Sally adored my dad but she always believed that he only married her to get a mother for me. He was a junior surgeon working long hours and it was difficult for him to cope with a kid at the same time,' she told him. 'When he died, Sally worried that someone might try to take me away from her—'

'Presumably this adoption occurred before she took to the bottle?' Xan slotted in, his careless wording exasperating Elvi.

'Yes, but the point I'm trying to make is that, even in the midst of grieving for my dad, Sally was scared that I would be taken away from her because we weren't related by blood—'

A shapely black brow skated up. 'And presumably you feel that you owe her something for that devotion. Did you ever check the terms of your father's will?'

The insinuation that her adoptive mother could've had something to gain from adopting her set Elvi's teeth on edge but it struck her as typical of Xan's intensely cynical outlook on life. 'He didn't leave a will. He wasn't much older than you when he died from an aneurysm. Sally applied to adopt me because she loved me and wanted to keep me with her and Daniel.'

'Then it sucks to be you,' Xan could not resist saying, thinking about what he knew of alcoholic behaviour and how Elvi must've suffered throughout most of her childhood. How on earth, he marvelled, had she still contrived to form such an intense bond with her adoptive mother in spite of the woman's failings? Betrayed or cheated by anyone, Xan never forgot or forgave. He drew a line and if it was crossed, that was that.

'Well, it didn't, not always,' Elvi protested. 'There were good times even when things were tough and she was never a nasty drunk, never abusive or violent. We were lucky.'

Lucky? Xan swallowed back a derisive retort while he studied her animated face. She *loved* talking about her family, he noted, reckoning that he could use that to make her relax around him. Although, hadn't he *already* used it? She had sacrificed her freedom and her virginity to preserve her precious family and he had taken what she gave without a moment's hesitation.

It was a sobering conclusion and he fell silent, irritated by the conscience that had come out of nowhere at him the day before to destroy his peace of mind. Elvi was as foreign to him as an alien would've been, he conceded grimly. That happy-clappy, positive attitude, that self-less streak of loyalty and love a mile wide. But no doubt his conscience would give up the fight and die again through lack of encouragement.

'So, where in Greece are we going exactly?'

'Thira, the island where I was born, not the most exciting destination if you're into party-ing,' Xan pronounced, but his hard, dark eyes and his intonation could not hide his fondness for the place, Elvi noted with interest as she learned that what Xan said did not always match what she read in his voice or expression. He was inherently deceptive, calculating too, and far too clever for his own good, she reminded herself warningly, but she could not help remembering the man who had thought to drag Sylvia out at dawn to help Elvi pack for a society wedding because Elvi had not had a clue what to wear or of how hot it would be in Greece. Occasionally, he could be thoughtful and he could identify potential problems in advance in a way she could not.

'And to celebrate the occasion of your very first flight...' Xan murmured as the steward approached them with a bottle of champagne. 'I know you don't usually imbibe but surely *one* glass—?'

Rather overwhelmed by the gesture he had made, Elvi nodded vigorous agreement, keen to prevent him from sharing *all* her secrets with the cabin staff. Xan paid no heed to hovering employees when he spoke, being apparently so accustomed to their presence that they might as well have been invisible. She clasped the moisture-beaded flute of champagne, bubbles bursting and tickling her nose as she sipped and politely smiled.

'It wouldn't have felt the same with orange juice,' Xan asserted.

She almost disagreed, tempted to say that it was the thought behind his gesture that mattered most, only such a comment seemed too revealing when she considered it and instead she said nothing. She sipped her drink while Xan told her about the island of Thira and his family home there. Only the family aspect didn't seem to be on his radar because, while he told her that his grandfather had built the house and his father had extended it, he mentioned neither his mother nor his siblings again. He told her about the private beach where he had learned to swim, the freedom of exploring the island as a boy and it all sounded idyllic, not what she had expected when he'd admitted to his father's five matrimonial forays.

'You can't possibly be getting tipsy on one glass,' Xan said abruptly when she giggled like a drain at only the mildest of jokes.

'It was topped up,' she reminded him, holding her breath to try and kill the giggles that had foamed out of her in a spontaneous tide.

Long brown fingers twitched the glass from between her fingers and set it aside. 'I want you sober,' he told her.

'I am,' she insisted, leaning forward, bright blue eyes locked to his lean, strong features, pale white-blonde hair rippling round her heart-shaped face.

Xan shifted in his seat opposite her, raw arousal humming through his big powerful body with almost painful intensity. 'Let's be frank,' he breathed in a driven undertone. 'I want you any way I can have you—'

'That can't be true,' Elvi responded uncomfortably. 'I'm no show-stopper—'

'You stop *me* in my tracks,' Xan reasoned.

Colour drenched her cheeks but the strangest little spark of energy danced through her veins, quickening her heartbeat and her breathing pattern. Nobody had *ever* wanted her like that. She fed herself excuses about how she rarely got the opportunity to even meet men, but Xan had only seen her a handful of times in passing and he hadn't forgotten her again. That made her feel important, special and infinitely less ordinary because she reckoned Xan could have any woman he wanted.

'Ditto,' she conceded in an awkward mutter when he appeared to be awaiting a response from her.

And Xan laughed and leapt upright without warning to simply lift her out of her seat and tumble her down on his lap as he sat down again. 'Thought you were never going to admit that,' he growled with unashamed satisfaction.

For once she didn't begrudge him that satisfaction. 'I don't lie,' she murmured with pride.

'All women lie,' Xan declared, lifting big brown hands to frame her face, brushing her hair back behind her small ears, his potent amber eyes hot and golden and bright with hunger.

'No, we don't—'

'What weight are you?' Xan shot back at her. And she told him and he told her she couldn't possibly be that weight, standing up to set her down on her feet and lifting her again with a very funny fake grunt of effort that made her giggle helplessly. Xan mock-collapsed back into his seat still gripping her tight before hoisting her up on her knees to sit facing astride him, disconcerting her, killing her giggling fit.

'I wouldn't admit to being that heavy if I wasn't,' she pointed out more circumspectly, barely able to catch her breath that close to him, uneasy at the sudden intimacy, wondering how to remove herself back to her own seat without making a production out of it.

Xan stared down at her ripe pink lips and sur-rendered to the inevitable without an ounce of concern. He teased at that full lower lip, pressed them softly apart, darted, delved with enthusi-asm and felt every inch of her tighten and quiver with response against him. His fingers trailed up a slim silky thigh to the heart of her, teasing fingers sliding below her knickers to locate the most sensitive spot and dallying there to make her moan feverishly into his mouth.

Elvi knew she ought to tell him to stop but she couldn't fight the seduction of sensation engulfing her in a shimmying surge of intense pleasure. She trembled over him, breath caught in her throat, her heart pounding inside her with electrifying anticipation. She squirmed as he stroked and teased and what she had believed she would never welcome again, she suddenly wanted with ferocious intensity. She buried her face against his shoulder, frantically breathing in the familiar scent of his skin, pressing her mouth against the strong brown column of his throat until his other hand caught into her hair to yank her head up. He drove her soft lips apart with a savage kiss of sizzling hunger at the same time as the tightening bands of tension in her pelvis sent her rocketing to her peak. Gasping, moaning, sobbing for breath, she came apart in his arms, shattered into so many pieces she barely recognised herself any more.

Xan settled her back into her seat and, although he was hugely aroused, his frustration was soothed by her explosive reaction to him. It was so honest, so *real*, like no connection he had ever had with a woman before and it excited him way beyond his experience. As Elvi focused on him in a daze of post-climactic bewilderment, as if she didn't quite know what had happened to her, Xan awarded her a dazzling smile of appreciation.

'Later, *moli mou*,' he savoured with growly masculine satisfaction.

CHAPTER SEVEN

NOTHING COULD HAVE prepared Elvi for the startling effect of Xan's mother, Ariadne, whose temperament was so very different from her only child's.

A helicopter had delivered Xan and Elvi to the huge sprawling white villa that overlooked a wooded cove on the island of Thira. As she climbed out a small woman accompanied by a pack of dogs stood up from a seat on the wide front terrace and came hurrying down the steps to eagerly greet them, dogs leaping and bouncing in concert. And from that moment, Elvi doubted that even Xan had managed to get a word in edgeways, for Ariadne talked in a constant stream, hopping confusingly from one topic to the next. She spoke fluent English, however, relieving Elvi's main fear that Xan would be the only person around who understood her, and the older woman was both friendly and welcoming.

On the way through the opulent house, Elvi received a stream of information. Ariadne's mother had been English and Ariadne did not normally live in the big villa, having her own home in the village by the harbour. But when Xan entertained the wider family, Ariadne always acted as his hostess.

'First wife seniority!' Ariadne joked. 'Xan doesn't like his stepmothers much but he accepts his brothers and sisters and, naturally, Delphina wanted her wedding staged here and her brother doing the service—'

'Her brother's a priest?'

'Lukas is a Greek Orthodox priest and Tobias, the other son, is gay. Not that I'm criticising, but Xan did turn out more conventional than his brothers,' Ariadne proclaimed with pride. 'And it goes without saying that he's the cleverest. Delphina's a dear, you'll love her. She and

Takis fell in love at school, almost like Helios and me… Xan's father, you know. But of course, Helios and I didn't attend the same school. I was the village doctor's daughter and we met when he went fishing. Like Xan, Helios was gorgeous.' Ariadne loosed an extravagant sigh as if she was looking back in time before continuing briskly, 'But he was also weak and unreliable and quite unable to keep his trousers zipped. Not very good at making money either. By the time Helios passed he had even mortgaged this house. Xan rescued all of us from penury.'

'Xan's…' Elvi hesitated as the eyes of Xan's mother locked with fixed attention to her face. 'He's quite a character,' she pronounced lamely.

The older woman showed the way into a bedroom where confusion seemed to have broken out between two maids over Elvi's luggage. Ariadne smiled even wider and rested a supervisory hand on Elvi's arm to guide her away from the small domestic dispute they had interrupted.

'Do you *know* how many years I've been waiting for my son to bring a woman home with him?' she asked earnestly.

'Oh…' Elvi reddened. 'Xan and I are not… er, serious or anything like that,' she hastened to declare.

'Xan doesn't know *how* to do serious. Not after witnessing the sort of shenanigans he grew up with in this house…all those wives, the live-in lovers who didn't make it to the altar, the screaming dramas,' Ariadne told her with scorn. 'All Helios's children suffered but Xan was older and he endured the most.'

Elvi frowned. 'He lived with his father, not you, after…er…the divorce?'

'Helios refused to give up custody of his eldest son. I was distraught. Losing your husband to another woman and then losing your only child at almost the same time was a huge shock for me.' Ariadne paused in the sunlit corridor lined with magnificent paintings, her rounded but still attractive face full of remembered pain and regret. 'I was young and heartbroken but I was also selfish. I walked away to make a fresh start instead of staying on the island and accepting that I could only be a part-time mother to my son.'

Elvi was listening closely, deeply interested in what she was learning about Xan's childhood. 'Walked away?' she encouraged, impatient to hear more.

But Ariadne, who had paused on the threshold of a much larger and more magnificent bedroom than she had previously shown to Elvi, was no longer looking at her. She was studying her son and she addressed him in Greek, her attitude one of humour while Xan stood there, his tall, powerful figure rigid, his bronzed face impassive, responding to the older woman with a noncommittal shrug that nonetheless telegraphed a temper on a short fuse to Elvi's increasingly observant eyes. Faint dark colour edged his killer cheekbones, a gleam of hot gold brightening his gaze.

'I will leave you with your...*friend.*' Xan's mother laughed in emphasis, standing back as Elvi's cases were brought in. 'Dinner is in an hour.'

Xan strode out onto the balcony that over-looked the sea. The Aegean Sea, almost as blue as Elvi's eyes, he brooded grimly, exasperated by his mother's infantile game-playing.

'So...' Elvi hovered uncertainly by the glass doors. 'What was that all about?'

Xan swung back, lithe as a jungle predator and as immaculate as he had been at dawn that morning, shirt still crisp and white, tie still straight. No, he badly needed a shave, she noted with relief, grateful he wasn't quite perfect when the linen sundress she had worn from travelling was as creased as though she had slept in it and bore a coffee stain.

'I haven't brought a woman to the island with me before.'

'I know. Your mother said.'

'To prevent her from reading too much into your visit, I said you were just a friend—'

'I said we weren't serious,' Elvi hastened to add.

'But Ariadne called my bluff,' Xan admitted, his beautiful stubborn mouth curling with annoyance. 'She put you in another room and naturally I countermanded that instruction.'

Elvi inwardly cringed and her cheeks reddened with embarrassment. In a household with other guests, all of them presumably Xan's relatives, staying in *his* room put her under the spotlight more than she would've liked, had she had a choice. And she didn't *have* a choice, she reminded herself ruefully.

'Ariadne's desperate for me to get married and produce grandchildren for her,' Xan revealed in an aggrieved undertone. 'But I'm nowhere near ready for that step.'

Elvi shrugged a stiff shoulder. 'Well, I imagine you'll do exactly as you like anyway and she knows that.'

Always throwing oil on troubled waters, that was Elvi, Xan noted, and it was a novel approach to a man quick to impatience and anger, but rather soothing to be around, if you needed to be handled as though you were an unstable explosive device. Was that how she saw him? To his own surprise, he asked her that question.

'Well, you're naturally intolerant,' Elvi pointed out almost apologetically, as if the unlovely trait of intolerance could not possibly be his own fault. 'You are very precise in your expectations and accustomed to other people meeting those expectations, either because you're paying them to do so or because you're used to people going out of their way to please you.'

'Both,' Xan agreed, impressed by her honesty and her tact. He didn't think he had ever been insulted or criticised so politely. 'Are you planning to go out of your way to please me any time soon?'

Elvi stiffened, her cheeks flushing, her mouth compressing. 'Probably not.'

Xan swung away to hide his smile because she would assume he was laughing at her and he wasn't. She was teaching him almost as much as he was teaching her and by the time she learned and accepted that sex was merely sex, he would probably be bored, he told himself stubbornly, striving to ignore the reality that simply the thought of getting her into the same bed at the end of the tedious evening ahead sent a throbbing, stabbing pulse of raw erotic craving through him. She would have an enjoyable holiday on Thira and then he would send her home. She would be restored to happy-clappy positivity, merely a little less innocent and the sordid aspects of their original arrangement would be tidily airbrushed over into something more acceptable.

Unaware of Xan's plans for her immediate future, Elvi smoothed down her dress, black, fitted with a lower neckline than she liked, but undeniably elegant.

'Wear your diamonds,' Xan advised, emerging from the bathroom in all his naked glory, so tall and bronzed with powerful pectorals and taut ropes of muscle visible across his flat abdomen.

With difficulty, Elvi dragged her eyes from that view, her body uncomfortably warm despite the air conditioning. 'They're not *my* diamonds—'

'I bought them for you.'

'I don't want them.'

'But you can *wear* them when I tell you to,' Xan cut in, flipping open the jewel case to extract the necklace and anchor it round her throat while she struggled to lift her hair out of his path.

She had sworn she would not do as she was told but here she was doing it like everyone else around Xan, Elvi reflected angrily. 'I'm leaving them behind when we part—'

Xan shrugged an indifferent shoulder. 'And when do you think that might be?'

'A week?' Elvi looked at him hopefully.

And without warning, Xan felt a surge of rage splinter through him. It was that hopeful look that implied that she could not wait to regain her freedom and escape him. A woman had never ever shown Xan that expression before.

'No chance,' he countered succinctly, his attention involuntarily lingering on the voluptuous display of her breasts in the dress. It wasn't so much that the neckline was too low as that she had rather more than could be easily contained.

'My face is at *this* level,' Elvi told him thinly, all too well aware of where his scrutiny had strayed.

'Obviously I'm going to look… I love your curves,' Xan retorted squarely. 'But I think you should change into another dress. I don't want anyone else looking.'

Thoroughly irritated by being asked to change when she was fully dressed, but disliking even more having her chest on display, Elvi stepped back into the built-in closet where her clothing had been hung to rifle through the selection for another option. She yanked out the blue dress she had worn for the party he had taken her to and dug out a different bra to go with it, disappearing into the bathroom for the exchange, tossing over her shoulder, 'I don't see why it should bother you if anyone did look!'

Xan compressed his wide sensual mouth while he thought about that. He didn't know why the idea bothered him, but it did. Her glorious hourglass shape was eye-catching and he didn't want to share it. Fortunately, she was not one of those women, and he had met quite a few, who deliberately exposed as much flesh as possible in the hope of attracting more male attention.

'Much better,' Xan pronounced when she reappeared, flushed and slightly tumbled, to settle exasperated eyes on him. 'I hope the swimwear you have isn't too revealing—'

Elvi rolled her eyes as she stepped through the doorway into the corridor ahead of him. Even the most modestly cut swimwear made her look like an old-style pin-up girl, a fact that had put her off swimming sessions at a young age. 'So, interestingly, you have a prudish streak too,' she remarked snidely.

Still insulted by her enthusiasm for leaving him to return to her workaday, poverty-stricken existence, Xan refused to rise to the bait.

Downstairs, a crowd of guests were enjoying pre-dinner drinks and Elvi was introduced to Xan's relations. The bride-to-be, Delphina, was a pretty brunette with a ridiculously shy version of Xan's eyes while her mother was a brassy blonde, who loosed a sarcastic laugh of disbelief when Elvi, asked what she did for a living, mentioned her most recent employment in a craft shop.

'You see, Callista,' Xan murmured in the mildest of tones. 'Some women do choose to *work* for a living.'

'I would just have ignored her,' Elvi whispered in reproof as they moved away.

'I'm not a fan of turning the other cheek,' Xan retorted crisply. 'Callista lives off the rich men she sleeps with and she had no business sneering at you. It's a wonder Delphina has turned out as well as she has.'

'Sleeping with rich men to get by sounds very *much* like work to me,' Elvi dared.

Xan froze and glanced down at her with a sudden frown.

'Oh, I wasn't getting at you,' Elvi said with mock innocence. 'After all, I did it to keep my mother out of prison and off drink, which is rather different.'

'Skase!' Xan shot down at her in a raw undertone.

'Meaning?'

'Shut up…drop the subject,' Xan bit out furiously as he leant down to her level.

'Well, you really can't go around with that "one rule for me but a different rule for everyone else" take on everything,' Elvi pointed out helplessly.

'I can do whatever I like—'

'And it's thoroughly bad for you,' Elvi told him firmly.

Xan swore under his breath, inflamed by her sheer nerve. Why didn't she worry about offending him, as other women did? He stood by watching his mother introduce Elvi to his remaining sisters, noticing how animated the conversation between them all became. Of course, he should've expected that, he told himself calmingly. His sisters all lived in the real world, unlike his former stepmother, Callista. One sister was an engineer with her own company, another was a doctor, the third a happy housewife with four children, two of which were very cute five-year-old female twins. Another and stronger generation of his family, he labelled with satisfaction, for not one of his siblings exhibited the money-grabbing greed of his former stepmothers. Yes, he had bought them all houses and financed their business projects, but essentially his brothers and sisters were independent, falling back on his wealth only in times of misfortune.

They sat down to dinner. By that stage it was clear to Xan that Elvi had gone down like a prize trophy with his family because his mother was pumping her about her love of dogs, while the wretched untrained little beasts formed begging round their feet, and his sisters were chattering to Elvi as though she were one of the family. It was her friendly gene, Xan decided, only becoming perversely annoyed when Elvi disappeared off to see his mother's latest craft project, which he knew would be an absolute disaster. Ariadne Ziakis might be the acclaimed author of several very weighty archaeology tomes and a professor in her university department, but she was not talented with her hands.

'I was doing the stitch wrong!' his mother proclaimed when she returned to the table to drink her coffee. 'And this wonderful girl showed me how to do it and it was *so* easy when you know how…'

Ne…yes, Elvi went down with the family like award-winning chocolate.

Tobias, always timid, confided in Elvi about his latest relationship breakdown, when he could barely bring himself to acknowledge that he was gay to Xan's face. Lukas pontificated happily about worldly indifference to the suffering of refugees and revealed that he had met the woman he hoped to marry. One sister revealed that she was pregnant again, another admitted to a serious boyfriend. Xan watched in silent astonishment while his family opened up to Elvi in a way they never did with him. Delphina related the entire story of her humdrum relationship with Takis in the kind of detail that would send most people to sleep, but Elvi listened as if she were hearing the most romantic story she had ever heard.

Maybe she genuinely did think that sort of stuff was romantic, Xan reflected in awe as not even a giggle escaped Elvi when she heard about Takis's marriage proposal: harbour restaurant, family party, roses at the table, bended knee, so conventional Xan's teeth hurt with saccharine overload just listening. Elvi was *nice*, he decided, in the most flexible interpretation of that overused word. People blossomed around her, drawn by her sincere interest, warmed by her kind and optimistic outlook on life. She was the absolute antithesis of him, Xan decided.

'She's adorable. Put a ring on her finger fast,' his mother urged as she said goodnight to him.

'She's far too kind and caring for you,' his eldest sister, the engineer, opined. 'You'll probably make her miserable.'

'Oh, I just love Elvi.' Delphina sighed blissfully, very much the lovestruck bride the night before her wedding.

'Elvi would make a good wife,' Lukas, the priest, told him staunchly. 'She's a godly woman.'

'She's a pet,' Tobias pronounced with starry eyes as Xan identified Elvi by his mother's side, down on her knees petting the scruffy dogs. 'Such a good listener.'

Chilled by that amount of family enthusiasm, Xan accepted the accolades without comment and reclaimed Elvi from the pet contingent with difficulty. On the upper landing, she paused to study a portrait. 'Is that your father?'

'Yes,' Xan confirmed, his attention locked to her rather than the painting. Her dress exposed her slender spine, where he already knew the soft, smooth skin felt like silk, and the fine fabric below her waist outlined the ripe, rounded swell of her bottom. His libido kicked in with lusty fervour and he coiled his hands into fists of restraint. Everything was going to be different *this* time, he assured himself. There would be no grabbing, no rushing, no cutting of sexual corners.

'When did he die?' she asked, still looking at the canvas.

'Nine years ago.'

'You do look very like him,' Elvi conceded as she moved on, her heart skipping a beat as

Xan closed his hand over hers, engulfing her smaller fingers.

'Thankfully that resemblance is all we shared.' Xan thrust wide the door of his bedroom and she brushed against him, her face turning up, her eyes blindingly blue and bright above her soft full mouth, and that view cut through his self-discipline like a knife through butter.

Xan ran his fingertips lightly down the bare line of her spine and she trembled, suddenly fiercely aware of him, her body involuntarily awakening to his touch. He edged her back against the wall and stroked her hair back from her flushed face. 'Now tell me that you want me...'

Elvi dealt him a stubborn glance because only the champagne during the flight had forced that admission from her. 'You don't need the ego boost.'

'Why are you still fighting something so natural?' Xan demanded, as if she was being thoroughly unreasonable.

'It's not natural to me,' Elvi argued, struggling not to melt into the lean, powerful contours of his body as he penned her in by the wall. He was so warm and he smelt amazing, her nostrils flaring on the familiar scent of him. Her nipples prickled, swelling and tightening, and an edgy pulse beat between her thighs.

Xan could not credit how stubborn she could be. He could not fathom how a woman so seemingly soft and warm and eager to please those around her could then be so resistant when it came to pleasing him. 'You're only making this harder for yourself.'

Elvi was so tense as she fought her arousal that she was barely breathing, her small body stiff. 'I don't think so. This is who I am. If I changed that, I couldn't respect myself any longer.'

'Only you would care to think about such things,' Xan intoned thickly. 'This close to you, I can only think about how much I want you—'

He pushed closer, pressing her back against

the wall, and even through their clothes she could feel the hard, insistent length of him against her stomach. A jolt of hungry need took her by storm, drying her mouth, stealing her breath, sending her heart hammering. 'Xan…' she heard herself whisper almost pleadingly.

'Powerful, isn't it?' Xan husked, his hands bracing on either side of her head, his eyes a hot scorching gold enhanced by lush black lashes. 'So powerful you can't think of anything else.'

'You're teasing me,' Elvi said breathlessly, her fingers splaying across his shirt front, the heat of his muscled chest encouraging her hand to flex and the fingers to spread in something very like a caress.

Xan pulled her hand down to where he really needed her attention and her fingers traced his bold length through the fabric of his trousers, her shy fascination powerfully erotic. He wanted to rip off his clothes there and then and teach her everything she didn't know and, gripped by that image, he shed his jacket where he stood and yanked off his tie, unbuttoning his shirt with one hand, unzipping with the other.

It was as though Elvi's heartbeat had extended to thump through her entire body. She felt giddy, overexcited despite her nerves. Recognising Xan's feverish eagerness for her touch removed her fear of doing the wrong thing. That he could crave her caresses as much as she craved his was a revelation and a tremendous equaliser. She pushed down his boxers and found him, she glided her fingers up and down before she got down on her knees. He shuddered as she found him with her mouth and he arched his hips, groaning something hoarse in Greek. She swirled her tongue, tantalising, teasing while she stroked and cupped and savoured him. His hand tightened in her hair and then he yanked her back up to him, kissing her as though his life depended on that connection.

He cannoned off the corner of a dresser as he hauled her bodily over to the bed, stood her up, struggling with the backless dress and its complicated closure. There was a ripping sound as he simply lost patience and tore the fragile fabric down the middle. She looked up at him in shock.

'I can't wait...' Xan confided fiercely, flipping her round to unfasten the bra that anchored at her waist. 'What a strange contraption,' he muttered, his hands rising to mould the full swell of her breasts, tugging at her straining nipples and then ravishing her mouth with his again, his tongue plunging deep, extracting a startled cry of urgency from her.

They landed on the bed with a bounce and she had no idea how they had got there from the door. Xan ripped off his shirt and flung it aside, yanking off what remained of his clothing at the same time, his impatience unconcealed. He crawled up the bed like a lethal predator, golden eyes ablaze as he repositioned her to his satisfaction.

'No, not this time,' he censured when she tried to inch beneath the sheet. 'No barriers, no boundaries, *moli mou*. You're a work of art and I want to look at you.'

He was all male power and muscle sheathed in sun-kissed skin from his wide shoulders to his lean hips and strong thighs. The thrusting, potent proof of his arousal made damp heat rise at the heart of her.

'I promise to drive you out of your mind with pleasure,' Xan breathed with raw sensuality.

Sliding down the bed and parting her thighs to feast on her with his mouth, he took her entirely by surprise. She gasped, yanked unavailingly at his black hair, and then finally surrendered to wild sensation. He teased her with his skill, and her frantic tension grew and grew while the hollow ache between her legs became unbearable. She tossed and she turned and then she writhed, lost in the excitement until she soared to a glorious peak and the world splintered into a multicoloured shower of fireworks.

Xan grinned down at her bemused face and sank into her with one powerful thrust. His groan of sheer unalloyed pleasure made her feel even hotter. This time her body craved him and she was much more relaxed and there wasn't even a hint of discomfort, only the wonderful rolling tide of exquisite sensation as his every movement sent smouldering pleasure winging through her.

'Don't stop,' she gasped at the height of another peak, every nerve straining greedily for more.

And Xan laughed with pure unashamed enjoyment, pulling back from her briefly to flip her over onto her knees to continue, driving deeper into her receptive body with every cry he wrenched from her until finally Elvi reached the highest summit of rapturous excitement and a seething rush of convulsive delight sent paroxysms of electrifying pleasure travelling through her exhausted length.

'Please don't make me move until tomorrow,' she mumbled, face down on the bed.

'I thought you were into cuddling.'

'Are you hot and sweaty?' she asked prosai-
cally.

'You want me to shower first?'

Elvi turned back over and laughed with helpless appreciation. 'Only joking!'

Xan closed an arm round her and pulled her
close. It wasn't a hug or a cuddle but it was more
of a connection than he had offered before and
it soothed her racing thoughts and the anxiety
she was holding at bay.

'You used a condom, didn't you?' she checked
worriedly.

'Of course. Are you still worrying about that?'
he said in surprise.

'Worrying comes naturally to me,' she admitted.

'Worrying is a waste of energy that can be
better employed. I want to have you again,' Xan
confided, pressing a kiss to a sensitive pulse
point below her ear, making her squirm.

'Already?' she gasped, huge blue eyes lifting
to his lean, darkly handsome face, instantly re-

joicing in the sleek dark beauty of him laced with the wilder elements of his tousled hair and stubble.

Xan nodded very seriously. 'I've got a major backlog of Elvi hunger to clear. I'm going to be very demanding, *moli mou...*'

A little flame of anticipation kindled wickedly low in her pelvis at that news. For the first time Elvi acknowledged just how much she revelled in Xan Ziakis, clothed or unclothed. It didn't matter how much he infuriated her, it didn't stop her craving him with every fibre of her being. It was only physical attraction, nothing more serious, she told herself with determination, telling herself to move with the times and stop judging herself for a situation she couldn't change. After all, their arrangement wouldn't last for ever and the real world would reclaim her soon enough.

Before she'd met Xan, she had sunk into a rut and stopped thinking about her own future, she acknowledged ruefully. Perhaps Joel had had a point when he'd criticised her for her absorption in her family. When Xan moved on, she decided that she would change her attitude. She would seek a more challenging job or even training that would enable her to be more ambitious. Her mother and brother were finding their own feet now and would no longer need to rely on her to the same extent.

When Xan emerged from the bathroom, Elvi was fast asleep. He had to fight the temptation to wake her while he studied her with brooding disquiet. Sex had never been so intense for him and his voracious desire to have her again disturbed him. He wasn't treating her the way he normally treated a mistress. He didn't know what it was about her that got to him deep down where he had sworn never to let a woman go again.

And inexplicably and unnervingly, she made him keep on changing his mind. What had happened to his determination not to touch her until she invited him to do so? What had happened to his decision to let her go free in five days?

Even worse, Elvi made him want more and he liked that even less.

Was it the fact that he was her first lover? Did he somehow feel responsible for her now? He reminded himself that he had wronged her and that he had deliberately set out to redress that damage. But that didn't explain why he hadn't just let her go or why he was tempted to put his arms around her when she was asleep and there was no chance of sex. *Thee mou…*that urge was freaking him out! He was even more unsettled by the tangle of clothing untidily littering the bedroom floor. That wasn't like him either. He was quick to remove the evidence of his lack of patience and control, but throughout the exercise he was acknowledging that he should not allow any woman to affect him the way she did and he was urging himself to walk away fast.

Elvi drifted slowly out of a deep sleep to greet the dawn. Light was filtering through the curtains and she was too warm. She muttered a complaint and the sheet was tossed back, Xan's fingers returning to the place which made her writhe and heat up even more. A slight gasp escaped her as he shifted against her, all power and potency and temptation and then he was where she needed him to be, sinking into her welcoming body with urgent force. But then the tempo changed to sensually slow and her tension ramped up accordingly, heart hammering with frantic longing, her body gripped by fierce, needy impatience. She pushed back against him, wanting, needing, and with a husky sound of appreciation, he speeded up, delivering what her body was programmed to crave in a heart-stopping, blood-stirring storm of sensation that peaked and then left her floating.

'I ordered breakfast in bed for you,' Xan murmured lazily. 'I have some work to catch up on before I have to walk Delphina into the church.'

'It'll take me all my time to get ready for the wedding,' Elvi sighed, feeling like a hot sweaty mess even while her whole body purred with little aftershocks of pleasure.

Xan strode out of the shower and she watched him dress, her brow furrowing while she ate. He seemed very preoccupied, his dark classic profile taut, his stunning eyes veiled. Something had changed, she grasped on a level she didn't quite understand: there was something different about Xan. A distance she hadn't noticed the night before? The first hint that their arrangement was already heading towards its natural end? Was he getting bored with her? It was what she wanted, what she *needed*. She had to pick herself back up and get her life back on track. Unfortunately, that did not clarify why her skin chilled and her tummy succumbed to a nauseous lurch at the thought of their parting.

There was no way she was becoming attached to Xan, she reasoned with firm conviction. She wasn't that foolish or that quick to allow her feelings to control her. At heart she was sensible and practical and a stranger to the kind of dangerous emotions that were likely to upset her. For goodness' sake, she had only been with him a few days, long enough to learn that sexual pleasure was a lot more seductive than she had ever dreamt but nowhere near long enough to start thinking too warmly of a man she disliked.

And she *did* dislike him, she *thoroughly* disliked him, Elvi reminded herself with satisfaction. Xan was immoral and unscrupulous and he expected the whole world to revolve around him and his needs and wants. All he cared about was making money and maintaining a stress-free sex life. They weren't even *in* a relationship. Everything Xan did and said spelled out that message because he didn't want her to misinterpret an intimacy that was not destined to last.

The sooner it was over between them, the better it would be for her, she told herself staunchly. She had changed as well. She would never be so naïve or trusting again. But that made her stronger rather than weaker…didn't it?

Two hours later, Elvi was garbed in an elegant

dark green dress and accompanying Xan's eldest sister, Hana, and her family to the village church. A former monastery, the large church sat at the heart of a very picturesque little village overlooking the harbour. The pews were packed, even though Hana had said that Delphina had wanted a very small wedding attended only by relatives. Elvi's attention was fully engaged taking in the wonderful painted ceiling and icons that made the candlelit church interior so colourful and warm. And then beside her, Hana said something abrupt in Greek and turned her head to look at the woman smilingly taking what appeared to be the last available seat in the row in front of them.

Hana's husband put his finger to his lips to silence the speech that was visibly brimming on his wife's lips as her dark eyes hardened with annoyance.

It wasn't the time or the place to ask who the woman was. She was certainly eye-catching, Elvi conceded admiringly, and evidently not bound by the tradition that suggested that only brides should wear white at a wedding. The brunette in the shimmering white dress was very tall, very slim and graceful and she had the face of an angel with big dark eyes, flawless features and a sultry pink mouth.

Elvi watched a sort of selective shimmy take place amongst the guests, heads turning as much as they dared, all eyes skimming in the direction of the late arrival, a low buzz of comment following. Clearly, whoever the woman was, her attendance was unexpected and food for a good gossip.

Xan dealt with the sudden appearance of the only woman who had ever broken his heart without batting a single eyelash. His first reaction was irritation, because even though Angie would have received an invite, being the bridegroom's cousin, she should have stayed away because Xan's family universally loathed her. His second reaction was that, although he despised her, she had worn well in their years apart.

When he received a lingering look of invitation from her, his inventive brain projected an image he very much liked. Two birds...*one* stone. Revenge and the freedom to move on in one perfect little package, he decided with ice-cold logic. Sometimes doing the right thing could mean doing it by nefarious means. It would be the wisest move he had ever made and would certainly kill at source his family's ridiculous conviction that he was ready to settle down.

CHAPTER EIGHT

'I'M SO SORRY about Angie showing up,' Delphina said, as though it were her fault that Xan's ex-girlfriend had decided to attend her wedding. 'Takis's mother insisted that it was only courtesy to send her an invitation but *nobody* expected her to actually come.'

'Why are you worrying about it?' Elvi asked gently. 'I'm not one bit bothered.'

It was a complete lie but Elvi had already heard enough about Angie Sarantos from Xan's worried family to last her a lifetime, and Delphina's embarrassment made her feel guilty because every bride had the right to enjoy her wedding day free of all such concerns.

Apparently, Xan had met Angie when he was twenty-one and had asked her to marry him. Angie, however, had ditched him once it became clear that the Ziakis family was in serious debt following the death of Xan's father. Within months she had married another man and moved to Switzerland to live and she was now a childless widow. Ariadne, Xan's adoring mother, was convinced that Angie was broke and on the prowl for a wealthy second husband. But Xan was no fool, Elvi reflected wryly. She just couldn't see him falling for the charms of an obvious gold-digger.

But if that was true, what *was* he playing at? He had not neglected Elvi in any way. He had sat beside her throughout the wedding breakfast staged back at the villa and had made very polite conversation, much as though they were chance-met strangers, rather than lovers. But once they were freed from their table and able to mingle, Xan had continually drifted in Angie's direction, pausing to chat with the other woman at every opportunity, laughing and joking with her as if she were his long-lost best friend. Old friends catching up and able to relive fond memories now that their parting was well behind them?

Maybe so, but Elvi had also noticed the cool distance of Xan's altered attitude towards herself and, whatever else that change denoted, she was convinced that he had decided that they were over. Why else would he behave in such a way? Besides, Angie Sarantos was absolutely stunning and Elvi knew she couldn't hold a candle to her.

How any man could travel so fast from wanting her passionately only hours earlier to flirting madly with his ex, she had no idea. But then she wasn't a transitory sort of person, was she? What she *did* feel, she felt deeply and the sentiment stayed with her. Xan, however, had only felt lust for her, nothing profound or more lasting.

Bearing those realities in mind, why did she currently feel as if she had been punched in the stomach? Why was she in shock? Why was she *hurt*? Where had those responses come from?

In truth she hurt as much as if Xan had taken a hammer to her heart and smashed it to pieces and she hated herself for that anguished sense of rejection and disillusionment, when instead she knew she should've been celebrating the prospect of returning to her own life, the life he had so ruthlessly yanked her out of.

Clearly, beneath the surface show of her hostility, she had contrived to become more emotionally attached to Xan than she had been prepared to acknowledge. That shamed her and put her on her mettle to appear untouched by the little drama of the flirtation that every other wedding guest appeared to find a source of fascination. You couldn't fall in love with anyone that quickly, she reasoned angrily with herself; it just wasn't possible. Possibly her pride was hurt, that foolish part of her that had unwisely revelled in Xan's seemingly overwhelming desire for her ordinary self. Pride cometh before a fall, she reminded herself studiously, trying to keep a smile pinned to her lips, struggling to stop her gaze tracking Xan or Angie round the room.

For that reason, it was a surprise when Xan appeared at her side and suggested they dance. Elvi gave him a pained glance and shook her head. 'No, thanks,' she said quietly.

She was pale, her eyes shadowed and for a split second Xan's resolve almost faltered, but the growing conviction that he was finally doing what he should've done some days earlier held him fast. He *had* to let her go: nothing else was acceptable and dragging out the process would be unnecessarily cruel.

'Go off and enjoy yourself… I'm quite tired,' Elvi insisted, not wanting his company if he was only putting on a show for the sake of appearances.

'If you're sure…' Xan straightened back to his full height, avoiding a meaningful look from his brother, the priest, that warned him that Lukas was in the mood to preach. Aware of his family's censorious appraisals, Xan decided it was time for a break to take care of some work and when the event was at an end he would speak to Elvi about her departure.

Alone again, Elvi walked outside onto the terrace and sat down, ostensibly to take in the panoramic view of the island and the sea. But she couldn't see anything but Xan inside her head, sleek, darkly beautiful Xan with his dazzling eyes laughing with her, smiling with her, filling her with feelings that felt so natural to her that she had not even realised that she was falling for him.

Angie Sarantos strolled out with a champagne goblet cradled nonchalantly in one slender hand. 'He's bored with you,' she murmured softly.

Elvi clenched her teeth hard. 'Are you speaking to me?'

'I imagine you hate my guts,' Angie remarked. 'But Xan and I have something special. I didn't know how special it was until I lost it. Point is, I made a mistake nine years ago and I know it.'

Elvi was reluctant to engage with the brunette in any way. 'It's none of my business—'

'It's not,' Angie agreed. 'But I won't let anyone come between me and Xan.'

Elvi's phone vibrated with a text and she pulled it out as an excuse and stood up. 'Excuse me, I have to take this—'

Stepping back into the cool air-conditioned interior, Elvi read the text from her mother and a wave of dizziness ran over her, perspiration beading her upper lip. Her brother, Daniel, had been injured in a car accident and he was in hospital. Suddenly, Elvi was desperate to get home and be with her family.

'Are you all right?' Hana asked her worriedly. 'You're as white as a sheet. Sit down for a moment—'

'No, I need to speak to Xan,' Elvi broke in apologetically. 'Do you know where he is?'

Minutes later, Elvi entered Xan's office on the ground floor. He was standing by the window, talking in French on the phone. Some words she vaguely recognised from school but most were incomprehensible as she hovered just over the threshold staring at him. For probably the *last* time, she reasoned numbly.

'I want to go home,' she declared shakily. 'My brother's in hospital.'

And from that point on, everything moved on oiled wheels. In fact, she had the feeling that Xan couldn't get her off the island of Thira fast enough because he could not have been more helpful. He insisted that she travel back on his private jet, instructed the staff to pack for her while also informing her that he had organised accommodation in London for her and that he would place money in her bank account.

'But I don't need accommodation or money!'

'Of course, you do,' Xan overruled without hesitation. 'It's my fault that you don't have employment to return to and you need support to get back on your feet again. The apartment you originally moved into is up for sale at present, so naturally I will provide somewhere else for you to stay.'

And at that point Elvi simply stopped arguing because arguing with Xan was exhausting. He would regroup and address the topic from another angle, usually one she hadn't yet thought of. What did strike her like a blow was his eagerness to speed her on her way and ease her passage with his wealth.

'You don't need to feel guilty that we're over,' Elvi told him abruptly, the reproof literally leaping straight from her brain onto her tongue. 'We didn't suit. We're like oil and water—'

Xan froze, his lean, powerful physique pulling taut, and his magnificent eyes flashed pure gold. 'I'm not feeling guilty. Why would I feel guilty?'

Her stomach already rolling with nausea, Elvi decided not to mention Angie. Why go there when she didn't have to and her family emergency had given Xan a ready excuse to move her back *out* of his life again as fast as he had dragged her into it?

'Look after yourself,' Xan urged grimly. 'And if you ever need anything, call me—'

Elvi dealt him a rueful grimace. 'Like that's going to happen,' she derided with newly learned cynicism. 'Goodbye, Xan.'

'Daniel's going to be fine. Your mother says he looks like he's been beaten up and he's sprained his ankle but that's all, so you don't need to worry,' Dmitri declared, letting her know that he too was in regular contact with her parent as he accompanied her out to the helicopter waiting in the grounds of the villa. 'I hope you know you're very welcome to move to Oxford with your family—'

Elvi smiled warmly at the older man. 'Thanks. I'm going to tell Mum the truth when I get back, well…*almost* the truth,' she adjusted with a slight wince. 'I won't tell her anything that upsets her.'

At noon the next day, after a sleepless flight on Xan's opulent jet and a harried arrival at yet another very fancy apartment, where she left her luggage stacked, Elvi went straight to the hospital and met her mother in the waiting area. Her eyes were burning in her head from exhaustion and the battle to stay in control of her emotions. *It's over.* The phrase kept on crashing into her head like an alarm bell shrilling and lacing her every thought with far too much drama. No, no, I'm *not* in love with him, this is a crush, a long-overdue crush and it *is* manageable, she told herself firmly.

'You were with Mr Ziakis…in *Greece*?' Sally Cartwright repeated in disbelief. 'What on earth—?'

'I went to see him after you were arrested and…then we had dinner and somehow we ended up getting involved,' Elvi admitted starkly. 'It was crazy and it all happened terribly fast…of course, it was never going to last—'

'But that's why he dropped the theft charge, I

imagine.' Her mother wrapped her arms round her trembling daughter and muttered soothing things, seeing far more than Elvi would ever have admitted in the hollowness of the younger woman's eyes and her drawn pallor.

The lies swept away, Elvi hoped she would feel better but her mood remained flat as a pancake. As Dmitri had forecast, Daniel was fine, his face badly bruised and swollen and his ankle sprained. Her sibling would be returning home with them on crutches.

Two weeks dragged past. Dmitri hired a van and moved Sally's family to his terraced house in Oxford. The property was beautifully renovated and a vast improvement on their previous home. Elvi finally got her own bedroom while her mother enthused about the freedom of having a garden again. Elvi, however, had more pressing things on her mind because her period was late. In a sombre mood, she went out to buy a pregnancy test, anxiously counting days on her fingers, striving to be optimistic as she recalled Xan's lack of concern over that contra-ceptive mishap.

Thinking about Xan only upset her and she tried not to do it but late at night, lying sleepless in bed, there was nothing else to think about. Xan hadn't had to say the words in the end but he had found her wanting and he had dumped her like an old shoe within days of taking her to bed for the first time. Her self-esteem at rock-bottom, Elvi threw herself into organis-ing their new home with her mother and look-ing up training courses online in an attempt to find something that truly interested her rather than settling for the first job available. Unhap-pily, the pregnancy scare hit her like an express train just when she was trying to move beyond heartbreak.

She sat in the bathroom clutching the wand before she even went downstairs to breakfast. Her brain was running at a thousand knots a minute. How *could* she be pregnant? How could a single oversight result in such a life-changing event? Yes, she knew the facts of life, but her hazy recollection of that first time with Xan seemed more about passion than anything else. The confirmation of a positive test came up and, in a panic, she reread the instructions all over again. She felt sick and dizzy, overwhelmed by fear of the unknown. She was pregnant, she acknowledged in shock; she was actually going to have Xan's baby.

She dragged in a steadying breath of oxygen. Naturally she knew there were alternatives but the idea of surrendering her baby to adoption had no appeal for her and she couldn't bring herself to consider a termination. She would have to tell Xan because he had the right to know: this was his child too. Before she could lose her nerve, she pulled out her phone to text him.

I need to see you. Something to tell you.

Xan read the text in the middle of a meeting. *Elvi.*

Meet for lunch?

His intelligence warned him that lunch was a very bad idea. Going cold turkey to kill an obsession was a basic ground rule. His hunger for Elvi was persistent, there in the morning when he awoke, there at night when he tried to shut down his thoughts and sleep. Somehow Elvi and her glorious curves had become an obsession, rarely out of his mind. What the hell would she want to see him about? Probably some problem relating to her family, he reasoned grimly, recalling that he *had* urged her to contact him at any time and could hardly complain if she had decided to take him up on the invitation.

Can't make it to lunch in time. Living in Oxford now.

Xan froze. She wasn't even occupying the apartment he had bought her? What the hell was she doing in Oxford? He asked her to meet him that afternoon at her apartment, the one she *wasn't* using, he clarified with controlled sarcasm.

It was ages before she assented with a grudging OK and promised to text him once she had worked out what time she would be there.

Elvi wouldn't allow herself to dress up for her meeting with Xan. He was the father of her unborn child, *not* a lover, *not* someone she wanted to impress, not anything really. In jeans and a purple filmy top, her hair confined in a long braid that snaked down her slender spine, she caught the train and battled every intimate memory that tried to sneak back into her mind. But she had forgotten nothing about Xan from the way he liked to check stocks and shares and eat in silence over breakfast to the provocative blaze of his stunning golden eyes when he was hungry for her.

Had he reconciled with Angie Sarantos? Or had that flirtation simply been a symptom of his restive boredom in Elvi's company? She allowed herself to think along those lines because it was realistic thinking and naturally she was curious. It was also best not to dwell in advance on Xan's likely horror at the news that she had conceived because she was well aware that he had not seriously entertained that possibility.

She texted Xan as soon as she arrived at the apartment and anxiously paced the living area while she waited. The shrill of the doorbell took her by surprise because she had assumed he would have a key for the second apartment as he had had for the first.

'Don't you have a key?' she asked as she pulled open the door and fell back a step.

'No, this apartment is in your name. I have no right of entry here,' Xan told her quietly.

'Are you saying you *bought* it for me? An *apartment*?' Elvi gasped incredulously as she went into instant retreat, intimidated by the height of him towering over her that close. Nor could she believe what she was hearing. He had moved her out of the other apartment to put her into a new one but she had no idea why. In any case, why on earth would he buy her an apartment?

Xan jerked a casual shoulder, dismissing the guilty conscience that had powered the purchase. 'I wanted you to be secure—'

'But you don't buy someone you barely know an apartment!' Elvi bleated, so disconcerted by what he had told her that she could think of nothing else. 'Obviously I assumed you'd rented it for me and I planned to let you know that I was back living with my family, only I hadn't got around to it yet....'

Xan wasn't listening although his attention was locked to her. He noticed that she had gone back to wearing her own clothing, tacitly rejecting the new wardrobe he had also given her, but just at that moment he didn't care. Indeed, given even the most minimal encouragement, he would have carted her off to the bedroom, unbraided her beautiful hair and laid her out like a banquet for his delectation. One look at her flushed face, evasive blue eyes and the curves no top in creation could have concealed and he was painfully aroused and...*and* obsessed again? He froze and then swung round to close the door behind him, utilising that moment to suppress his baser urges.

'You'd better come in,' Elvi muttered belatedly. 'I've got something to tell you—'

Xan moved warily to the threshold of the living area and lodged there, carefully maintaining his distance. 'So, tell me... I sent my limo round the block. I wasn't expecting to be here for long.'

'I'm... I'm pregnant,' Elvi announced in a hoarse undertone.

Deprived of speech and reaction for possibly the very first time in his life, Xan stared back at her in unconcealed shock, his strong features tightening and paling as the gravity of her admission sank in on him.

'I wouldn't have got in touch with you again for anything less serious,' Elvi added defensively. 'You thought we didn't have anything to worry about but we *do*...'

'Yes, clearly,' Xan agreed, struggling to come to terms with her announcement at the same time as he came up with a solution. It was the way he worked. He saw a problem and he immediately set out to fix it and fast. A baby, the kind of little entity he had imagined would enliven his middle age, rather than his wild-oats-sowing years. Bang went his perfectly planned future! But thinking on his feet was second nature to Xan and flexibility was a key skill. There *had* to be a resolution that would cover their situation.

'I don't want a termination and I don't want to put my child up for adoption either,' Elvi declared, deciding to lay all that out for him upfront before he got any ideas.

'I suppose the odds of conception were more promising than I was prepared to contemplate,' Xan commented reflectively, stalking deeper into the room as he pulled out his phone to let his driver know that he would be a while. 'I am one of seven children, after all.'

Her knees wobbling as her extreme tension faded, Elvi dropped down like a stone into a leather seat and clasped her hands tightly together on her knees. 'What are we going to do?'

'We're adults. We'll deal with it,' Xan asserted without hesitation.

Elvi resisted the urge to admit that she didn't feel much like an adult at that moment because she was in unfamiliar territory and apprehensive of a future as a single parent. Both admissions, however, sounded defeatist to her. Even worse, all the angst in the air was preventing her from taking any pleasure at all in her conception. Instead of feeling excited at the prospect of becoming a mother for the first time, she felt guilty, as though her body had done something it shouldn't have done.

Xan was thinking at top speed and already acknowledging that there *was* no magical solution to their plight. A child would be born, *his* child, *his* responsibility. But regardless of the support he gave to his child's mother, he would only be an occasional parent, who received scheduled visits. He would never be fully involved because he and Elvi would be leading separate lives.

And that would be where the problems started, he conceded reluctantly. He was very much aware of the consequences children suffered after a relationship breakdown when parents led separate lives. It had most often been Xan, as the eldest, who had been required to deal with his siblings when any of them had gone off the rails as adolescents. His father had been a useless parent, his priority always to move on selfishly to the next new woman in his life, leaving the children of his past relationships to sink or swim alongside their resentful, embittered mothers.

Xan knew he could walk away and be a parent from a safe distance, leaving Elvi to deal with the burden of childcare. But if he did that, he would be no better than the father he had despised. In any case, he *wanted* his child to have everything he and his siblings had been denied: stability and security and parents who watched over them. If he didn't want a parade of stepfathers or stepmothers disrupting his child's life he had to be tough and accept that he had only one sensible option open to him, he reasoned tautly. And unpalatable as the prospect of marriage might appear, there was, nevertheless, nothing more attractive to Xan in that moment of hard realism than the concept of having the right of unrestricted access to Elvi. For that benefit, he acknowledged, he was willing to make considerable sacrifices.

'We should get married,' Xan breathed harshly, shaken by the inescapable conviction that marriage offered a security for his child that he could not achieve by any other means.

'Don't be silly,' Elvi mumbled straight away, thinking he was trying to lighten the atmosphere with an ill-judged joke.

Xan settled hard dark golden eyes on her.

'Marriage is still the best framework in which to raise a child.'

'But you don't *want* to marry me!' Elvi countered impatiently. 'So why talk about it?'

'Let's not get into personal feelings,' Xan advised very drily, noticing her bra through the filmy top, his body tensing like a schoolboy's in response and decimating his pride. He swung away from that alluring view before continuing, 'More importantly, we now have a child's future to consider and we must do the best we can to ensure that our child enjoys the best possible start in life.'

Disconcerted by that unexpectedly serious assessment, Elvi glanced away from him uncomfortably. 'People don't get married just because they're parents these days. I'm amazed to hear you talking like this.'

'Elvi…' Xan exhaled in an impatient hiss. 'I'm talking like this because I *know* what I'm talking about! Children thrive only when they feel secure. In all the years I was growing up

I never felt secure because there was nothing stable about my home life. It was constant upheaval and change and I had no control over it. A new wife or lover would move in, turn the house on Thira upside down with different rules and then it would happen again…and *again*,' he told her in a roughened undertone, loathing the need to speak about such personal experiences.

'What you're really telling me is that even your father's many marriages didn't give you or your brothers and sisters security,' Elvi pointed out ruefully. 'So, how could us marrying possibly be the answer?'

Xan threw his arrogant dark head high, his jawline clenching. 'Unlike my father, I'm willing to make the effort for it to work.'

'But you said to leave personal feelings out of this and that doesn't work either because a marriage is based on two people living together,' Elvi argued. 'And I *couldn't* live with you.'

Xan stiffened in astonishment at that claim,

a winged ebony brow climbing. 'What do you mean? You *couldn't* live with me? Why not?'

The look of outrage in his stunning golden gaze failed to intimidate Elvi, who believed that any talk of Xan marrying her was total nonsense. 'Xan, have you forgotten how you behaved at your sister's wedding?' she asked tightly. 'You got bored with me within forty-eight hours and wasted no time in switching your interest to Angie. You're volatile—'

Xan gritted his even white teeth, incensed by the condemnation. He had had good reason to behave as he had but he was not prepared to share those reasons with her. 'I am *not* volatile,' he breathed, anger lacing his dark deep drawl with warning.

Elvi was tempted to tell him that possibly he bore more of a resemblance to his womanising father than he liked to think, but she resisted the urge because infuriating Xan would only create more problems. He couldn't really be serious about his suggestion that she marry him, she reasoned in bewilderment.

'You're just not the faithful type,' she said, unable to prevent that belief from leaping straight off her tongue. 'And I couldn't cope with that.'

Dark colour laced Xan's killer cheekbones. He was in a rage and battling to contain it. Women had been angling for a marriage proposal from him since he'd made his first billion. He knew that the lifestyle he could offer was his biggest attraction. He had always assumed that when he finally proposed he would be trodden on by his choice of bride in her haste to get him to the altar before he could change his mind. He had never once envisaged rejection. After all, Angie had been a different case, ditching him at a time when he appeared to be a poor financial bet. That Elvi could summarily dismiss him in the husband stakes as volatile and likely to be unfaithful incensed him.

'It may surprise you to know that I have *never* been unfaithful to a sexual partner,' Xan grated.

'My lovers don't overlap. I like clarity and candour in my personal life.'

Elvi coloured uncomfortably, wondering whether she could believe him. To be fair, he had been blunt with her from the outset about the limits of their arrangement. He had not told her any lies or broken any promises. But even so, his behaviour with his first love at his sister's wedding had *hurt* Elvi and continued to nag at her like a sore tooth. Perhaps she was too rigid in her outlook, not having had any former loves in her own past, she conceded ruefully.

Evidently, Xan had not seen Angie Sarantos since their breakup and naturally he had been curious. Furthermore, his familiarity with the other woman had only underlined the fact that they must once have been very close. Equally, there had been no sin in his enjoying Angie's company. There had been no stolen kisses, indeed nothing that Elvi could label an actual betrayal of trust. True, Angie had cherished a strong desire to win Xan back but Elvi could hardly blame him for the brunette's aspirations.

Elvi released her breath on a slow hiss. 'I was judging you and I shouldn't have been,' she admitted stiffly. 'The trouble is I still don't know you well enough to know if I can trust you.'

'You can surely trust that I want to do the best I can for our child,' Xan argued in a driven undertone. *'Thee mou,* Elvi…asking you to marry me was a major act of trust for me! And how else can we share our child? We *need* that framework… I'm not very good at sharing but if you're my wife, I will adapt.'

I'm not very good at sharing. That careless admission sliced through Elvi's thoughts like a blade and released a sudden flood of apprehension. Xan's father, Helios, had not wanted to share his child either. Although he had ditched his first wife, he had insisted on retaining custody of their son. How could she have forgotten that she was dealing with a man raised almost exclusively by his father?

And what if she too became superfluous to Xan's requirements? What if the way she chose to raise their child failed to meet his expectations? What if he decided that he wasn't seeing enough of his child? How many rights would she have as an unmarried mother on a low income? And how the heck would she ever contrive to fight such a very wealthy and powerful man?

Sheer panic at the threat of such future developments stirred nausea in Elvi's tummy and turned her entire skin surface clammy. Wives had more legal rights than single mothers, didn't they? Surely a wife could not be brushed aside in the same way? Out of pride and hurt, Ariadne had simply chosen not to fight her ex-husband for custody of her son, but Elvi knew that she would have fought to the death before surrendering her own flesh and blood. If such a battle ever became necessary, she decided that she *would* be safer and stronger as Xan's wife.

Xan scanned Elvi's troubled blue eyes and the

hands she was unconsciously twisting together on her lap. Guilt sliced through him. In using Angie as an excuse to extract himself from his affair with Elvi, he had done much more damage than he had ever intended. The consequences were only hitting him now. Elvi was wary, distrustful and reluctant to even *reach* for the security of a wedding ring. Angie would've grabbed the ring and laughed all the way to the divorce court and a fat financial settlement. But then, he conceded wryly, Angie and Elvi had barely a thought in common. He had only appreciated that contrast when Angie had sworn viciously at him when he'd told her that he wasn't interested in reliving their past after his sister's wedding. Angie had been enraged, not hurt. She was hard as nails, bitter over the choices she had made and as much a stranger to the softer, more feminine emotions as a rock.

With difficulty, Elvi dragged herself out of the freezing grip of extreme apprehension and drew in a slow, steadying breath before looking across at Xan. There was a brooding, distant look already etched on his lean, breathtakingly handsome features and she imagined manipulative wheels were already turning at speed in that dynamic brain of his because Xan was programmed to fight and win. If Plan A failed to deliver, he would waste no time in moving on to Plan B and heaven only knew what Plan B might entail.

'If you honestly believe that marriage would be the best option for our child,' she muttered shakily before she could lose her nerve, 'I agree.'

Xan studied her in astonishment because she had performed a one-hundred-and-eighty-degree turnaround in the space of minutes. 'You'll marry me?' he pressed with a frown.

'If that's what you want,' Elvi stated more firmly.

What had changed her mind? Xan scanned her with questioning dark golden eyes and then tossed pointless curiosity on the back burner. She would marry him and he would have both her and his child. For the moment that was enough, he told himself stubbornly. Did it really matter that she would want much more from him than any other woman ever had? Elvi would want him to change and cuddling would be the least of it. Ultimately, Elvi would want love and that worried him because he really didn't think he could give her love. He could be loyal and faithful but the thought of loving anyone, when everyone he had ever loved in life had either let him down or abandoned him, sent menacing cold chills running through Xan.

'The first thing we will do is visit a doctor to have your pregnancy confirmed,' Xan decreed. 'You'll come home with me to the penthouse tonight—'

'No. I'll stay with my family until we get married,' Elvi interrupted tightly, shying away from the thought of returning to that intimate setting with him. 'And if I agree to see a doctor, it has to be alone.'

'Let's not quibble about the details, *moli mou*,'

Xan urged softly, his spectacular golden eyes gleaming like priceless ingots as he appraised her, already trying to picture her swollen with his child. The image shocked him by turning him on hard and fast, something primal in him reacting to that concept with spontaneous vigour.

'I guess not,' Elvi muttered uncertainly, meeting the blaze of his scrutiny and stilling like a mouse suddenly scenting a predator stalking her. Colour banished her pallor, heat curling between her thighs in a wanton surge that embarrassed her. 'But there's something I should explain to you *before* you meet my family.'

Xan hadn't even thought of meeting Elvi's family. He had merely vaguely assumed that they would attend the wedding. Her mother, his former maid, he thought now with a faint shudder, and a thief into the bargain.

'It's time you knew the truth about the theft,' Elvi told him with determination.

CHAPTER NINE

XAN LISTENED IN stunned silence while Elvi told him the story about her kid brother's accidental removal of the brush pot from his penthouse apartment. Anger sparked, flared and climbed to an extraordinary height inside him.

'So, let me get this straight,' Xan urged with lethal derision. 'I was cast as the baddie in this scenario right from the start. You couldn't trust me with the truth, your mother couldn't and even my own head of security, who clearly worked out the truth from the beginning, couldn't trust me to do the right thing!'

'It wasn't like that, Xan—'

'It was *exactly* like that,' Xan retorted crushingly, his volatile temper flaring like a comet over the lowering awareness that everybody but him had known what was going on. 'You *all* presupposed that I would visit my wrath on your little brother and would refuse to believe his version of what happened.'

'We didn't want to take the risk that you would react the wrong way,' Elvi admitted heavily.

'*Diavole*…well, I'm reacting very much in the wrong way now!' Xan slung at her in a raw undertone. 'You all conspired to keep the truth from me.'

'No, that's untrue!' Elvi argued, leaping upright. 'My mother worked it out when the police found the brush pot in our home and she immediately owned up to protect Daniel. There was no discussion, no conspiracy and Dmitri simply *guessed* what had happened because he was there that day. I *had* to tell you before the wedding, Xan. I'm sorry you're annoyed but I couldn't let you go on believing that my mother is a thief.'

Still furious, Xan released his breath in a measured hiss even as he reflected that that word, 'annoyed', barely covered his reaction. Even as he controlled his scorching anger, however, he was understanding another, even less palatable side to what he had belatedly learned: he had taken his rage over the theft out on a complete innocent. Although no actual crime had been committed, he had intimidated Elvi into becoming his mistress. There was no escaping that harsh fact. His unjust treatment of her bit deeper than ever. His conscience would never be clear on that score because, not only had he railroaded a virgin into his bed, he had also been careless enough of her well-being to get her pregnant.

Xan's long brown fingers curled into potent fists of frustration. It was another dark day for him, he acknowledged bitterly. Was there to be no end to the constant revelations of his sins, his oversights, his *mistakes*? Had some greater force thrown Elvi into his path simply to trip him up and teach him that he was as fallible as every other human being? Cocooned by wealth and arrogance, he had believed he was untouchable and far too clever to be seduced by temptation. But one fatal moment of weakness had overwhelmed him with the kind of messy consequences he had successfully avoided all his life.

Elvi was that weakness and his inability to resist Elvi had directly led to the conception of his first child and would soon be followed by a shotgun marriage. Without warning, Xan was viewing life through a changed lens and feelings he had suppressed for years were surging to the fore and destabilising him. He didn't do self-doubt and castigation but Elvi's arrival had changed everything, transforming him into a man he barely recognised.

'You have my promise that in the future I will treat your family with every respect,' he ground out flatly.

'I appreciate that,' Elvi admitted quietly.

Xan gazed at her, hunger rising spontaneously from the ashes of his anger. He didn't understand how she could *do* that to him, make him flip from rage to a sexual craving so deep and strong it made him ache. He wanted to take her home with him and possess her over and over again until that ferocious, uncontrollable need was finally sated. And all that desire meant was that once again he was selfishly in the wrong because the unwitting object of his desire was pregnant and fragile.

Elvi met Xan's dark brooding gaze and butterflies leapt and danced in her tummy, emotions and responses she struggled to contain assailing her, making her feel hot and foolish and giddy. 'If it's any consolation, I'm sorry I didn't feel able to tell you the truth sooner.'

Possibly Xan didn't appreciate how daunting his reputation was or how frightening the amount of power he wielded could be, Elvi reflected ruefully. But the clenched set of his hard, dark face disturbed her, making her appreciate that Xan's emotions ran deep, much deeper than she had ever suspected. It was not that she had ever believed him to be shallow, but she had mistakenly assumed that his self-discipline kept his emotions fully in check. She could see, however, that he was still angry and upset, papering over the cracks to put her at ease, but still upset by her clear belief that he could not have been trusted to treat her little brother with understanding and compassion. And try as she might, that suspicion only made her want to hold him close and hug him, a response which would've been no more welcome to him, she conceded unhappily.

'You are sure that you want to go through with this?' Sally Cartwright prompted worriedly, her attention locked to her daughter's pale profile as she sat staring out of the window of the limousine. 'You *can* change your mind at the very last moment. I won't be upset.'

'I'm not having second thoughts. I'm just nervous.' Elvi forced a smile and tugged at the sleeves of her dress with restive fingers. It was a dream creation. Intricate embroidered lace sheathed her arms and ornamented the bodice, the classic shape moulding her figure while the slim skirt lent her an elegant tailored look.

'I've said it before and I'll say it again. Falling pregnant isn't a good enough reason to get married,' her mother continued. 'We would manage—'

'Xan wants this baby too,' Elvi reminded the older woman.

'He's a very reserved man, the exact opposite of the kind of man I always thought you would choose,' Sally admitted bluntly.

'Somehow we work,' Elvi parried uncomfortably, wishing her mother noticed a little less, knowing her subdued mood had encouraged Sally's last-ditch attempt to get her daughter to reconsider her plans.

In the two weeks since she had agreed to marry Xan, she had been very busy. Xan had come down to Oxford to meet her mother and her brother. He had been smoothly polite and pleasant but Elvi had recognised his discomfiture even if nobody else had. Everyone in her family had assumed the worst of him and he knew it.

He had hired a wedding planner to take charge of their big day. He had arranged for her to visit a designer salon, where she had fallen in love with her dress and where the staff had taken great care to ensure it was a perfect fit. He would've preferred her to move into the penthouse with him, but he had accepted her decision to stay with her family without argument. He had even accompanied her to the doctor to have her pregnancy confirmed and, since he had taken that time out of his day for her benefit, she had allowed him to join her for the consultation. In fact, in every way possible Xan had been supportive, reasonable and considerate of her needs. So why were her spirits low on her wedding day?

Possibly being forced to consider her future had also forced her to be more honest with herself. Once she had recognised Xan's emotional depth and his sheer determination to do what he believed to be right, she had finally acknowledged that she had fallen in love with him. He worked very hard at hiding his true nature behind a cold, indifferent façade and she wondered why he was that way, why he had felt the need to suggest that he had enjoyed an idyllic childhood when clearly, from the number of marriages his father had had, it must have been anything but idyllic. But Xan had only allowed her the glimpse of that harsh truth when he discussed what he wanted for his own child and admitted that he had never felt secure when he was a boy.

And ironically the reason she loved Xan was also why she was unhappy. In marrying her because she was pregnant, he was doing what he believed he *had* to do for their child's benefit. He didn't love her, wouldn't miss her if she was gone, wasn't marrying her for the *right* reasons, so how could she celebrate her wedding day? Even worse, he had not laid a finger on her since she had left the island, had stolen not so much as a single kiss, which scarcely suggested that she was the most sexually desirable of brides.

They arrived at the London church and she walked down the aisle on her brother's arm, wondering if her friend, Joel, was in the church. Joel had been acting oddly with her from the day he received the wedding invitation, phoning her up to demand to know when she had met Xan and why she hadn't mentioned that she was seeing someone. His apparent annoyance had been unfair when he had been up in Scotland and out of contact for weeks while he worked on a portrait commission. Elvi supposed that Joel's reaction was proof that some people really didn't like surprises.

Meeting Xan's mother, Ariadne's beaming smile as she reached the end of the aisle, Elvi went pink. Xan's family had greeted her with open arms and she was very grateful for that, even if she recognised that their hostility would not have made a dime of difference to Xan, who ruthlessly walked his own path. She finally let her attention focus on the tall Greek man awaiting her at the altar, the fine dark grey suit outlining his broad shoulders and lean, powerful physique, a ripple of compelling awareness shimmying through her before she even connected with his dazzling amber-gold eyes and the lush black lashes that so effectively framed them. Her tummy shifted and her heartbeat quickened as her mouth ran dry, liquid heat snaking wantonly up through her pelvis.

She wanted Xan, wanted him as she had never known she could want any man and it still unnerved her, that needy wanting, that treacherous hunger that transcended all barriers and had nothing to do with her brain. Her colour heightened, her legs weak, she swayed a little and he rested a steadying hand against the shallow indentation of her spine, the heat of his light hold leaving her insanely aware of his masculinity. Not cool, so not cool, she castigated her disobedient body as the ceremony began.

Xan threaded a slender platinum ring onto her finger, his touch sure, his responses firmer and clearer than her own, no hint of nervous tension in *his* demeanour. He was her husband now, she registered in awe, turning away from the altar with her hand resting on his arm. It was done now: they were married. *Because* she had conceived, not for any other reason, she reminded herself wretchedly, feeling like a ball and chain foisted on him, telling herself off for that fanciful thought. After all, they were both equally responsible for the contraceptive oversight that had led to conception.

All Xan's family had made a special effort to attend their wedding, even Delphina and Takis, who had cut short their honeymoon to spend a few days in London. On the steps, Elvi smiled and smiled until her face hurt with the effort of putting on a good show. Joel had come to the wedding, she noted with relief, seeing her best friend in the crowd, his mobile face unusually stiff and expressionless. Disapproving? Like her own family, he probably assumed she was rushing into marriage too quickly but then she hadn't told Joel that she was pregnant. Just then she wondered if Xan's family were aware of her condition and she asked Xan once they were in the limo travelling to the hotel for the reception.

His lean, darkly handsome features tensed. 'I saw no reason to mention it. The baby's our business.'

Relieved, Elvi nodded agreement, wondering if his family would have been as welcoming had they known the truth or whether she would have been downgraded to the level of a calculating hussy, who had entrapped Xan. Whatever, it scarcely mattered, she conceded ruefully, because they would realise that she was pregnant soon enough.

After the meal was served they circulated. She saw her mother chatting to Dmitri and noted Xan staring.

'What's going on there?' he asked drily.

'Nothing as yet, but give them time,' Elvi said

lightly. 'I shouldn't imagine Dmitri went to the trouble of offering my mother his house and setting her up with a job for no good reason.'

'You don't mind?' Xan queried.

'Mum's been on her own a long time. Does it bother you?'

Xan ignored the question, deep within his own thoughts. He blamed Dmitri for not sharing his doubts with him concerning Sally Cartwright's guilt. Had he known there were grounds for doubt, would he still have offered Elvi that iniquitous arrangement? He knew he was splitting hairs and was grimly amused by the fact. After all, no honourable man would have offered Elvi the option Xan had.

Joel signalled her from across the room and she left Xan's side with a warm welcoming smile. 'Thought you weren't sure you could come,' she greeted her old friend. 'I'm so glad you could make it after all.'

Joel dealt her a comprehensive appraisal, taking in the diamonds glittering in her ears and outlining her slender throat. 'You look amazing,' he told her thinly, curving an arm to her spine to guide her out to the bar, which was quieter. 'I'm glad sour grapes didn't keep me away—'

'Sour grapes?' she queried, not getting his meaning as he drew her into a secluded corner.

Joel sighed. 'You never did work it out, did you? You didn't notice what was right in front of you. I wanted you to turn to me when you were ready for a relationship but obviously I missed the boat—'

Elvi turned pale in shock and frowned at him in dismay. 'You don't mean that—'

Joel studied her in frustration. 'I always wanted you, even when we were at school… that's how far back it goes for me,' he admitted ruefully. 'When you didn't pick up on my signals, I told myself that it was because you were still immature and too wrapped up in your family but I've *always* loved you—'

Her tender heart was pierced by the vulnerable look in his eyes. 'I'm so sorry, Joel. I didn't realise—'

'You don't come to a wedding to tell the bride *that*,' Xan intoned harshly from behind Elvi and she spun round in consternation, disconcerted by his arrival.

'There's no harm in telling her,' Joel argued defiantly. 'After all, when you mess up, I want her to know I'm here *waiting* for her—'

Elvi froze in disbelief as Xan pressed her back out of the way with one arm and punched Joel with the other. Stunned by Xan's behaviour, she staggered back as Dmitri appeared out of nowhere to band his arms round Joel and restrain him when he tried to throw himself at Xan. There was a tough exchange of words between the men, but when Elvi went to Joel's side to apologise for the bridegroom's behaviour and check that her friend was all right, he told her angrily to leave him alone and he stalked out.

'What on earth did you think you were doing?' Elvi demanded of Xan.

Xan didn't have an answer for Elvi. Thumping the pretty boy with the dimples and curls had been instinctive and if his security team hadn't prevented further violence Xan would have enjoyed hitting him again. *And* again. How *dared* the little twerp? Who the hell was he anyway? Who had invited him? What sort of relationship did he have with Elvi? Xan wanted answers too.

'Who is he?' Xan bit out in a raw undertone.

'Joel is my best friend…and you *hit* him!' she condemned.

'Your best friend is a *man*?' Xan countered in disbelief. 'Well, that ends now. I'm not putting up with that kind of nonsense. You're my wife… you're *mine*. You don't let other men come onto you like that!'

Elvi was fit to be tied but she was conscious that people were watching them and she chose discretion, walking away and heading fast for the cloakroom.

Xan was tempted to yank her back because he was determined to hear the entire history of her involvement with Joel with no detail overlooked. Her best friend? How was he supposed to react to a crazy announcement like that? The sneaky little bastard had been telling Elvi that he loved her, trying to tempt her away when any decent man would have accepted the reality that she was newly married. Pregnant into the bargain, Xan recalled with sudden immense satisfaction.

CHAPTER TEN

ELVI BOARDED XAN'S private jet with a sense of liberation because the strain of the day and the pressure of being the centre of attention as bride and groom were now safely behind them. Being forced to act as though nothing was wrong between her and Xan after that incident with Joel had stressed her out. His aggressive reaction to Joel's declaration had shaken her and she knew she had to confront him. Violence would never ever be acceptable to Elvi.

'You still haven't told me where we're going,' she reminded Xan gently once they were airborne.

'The South of France. I have a house there that I rarely use. I did think of taking you back to the island, but my family wouldn't have given us much peace on Thira,' he told her wryly.

'I like your family,' Elvi protested.

'We need alone time,' Xan countered smoothly. 'That's your cue to start telling me about Joel…'

Elvi tensed and stirred her coffee. 'There's not much to say. We've been friends since primary school. He was so into art even then that he didn't fit in with the boys but I got on great with him. He's now making quite a name for himself as a portrait painter.'

'If you're that close, you should've told me about him,' Xan informed her disapprovingly.

'You should've told me about Angie,' Elvi countered without hesitation. 'She's much more relevant to this conversation than any we could have about Joel. Joel and I have only ever been friends. He's the big brother I never had.'

'Only it's obvious that he cherishes *far* from brotherly feelings for you,' Xan derided, his lean, strong face revealing not an ounce of discomfiture at her reference to his former girlfriend.

'He said he does but I still find that hard to believe,' Elvi confided, shaking her head in amazement. 'I have to admit that I didn't notice anything different in the way he treated me—'

Xan's wide sensual mouth quirked at that admission. 'You're not vain and you wouldn't have been looking for it. I saw how shocked you were. If I hadn't I would have been wondering if you had been involved in some relationship with him behind my back.'

Elvi's temper stirred at that insinuation and she lifted her chin and gave him a defiant look, her cheeks reddening. 'Surely you could hardly have wondered that when you became my first lover?' she dared. 'Please don't try to use *that* as an excuse for the violence you employed.'

'I'm not looking for an excuse. I'm not sorry I hit him,' Xan asserted immediately, springing upright to tower over her, the fine fabric of his tailored suit pulling against his strong muscular thighs and wide taut shoulders, distracting her when she least wanted to be distracted.

'There was absolutely no need or excuse for violence,' Elvi declared.

His lean bronzed features were taut and hard

as he helped himself to a drink at the integral bar. 'He crossed a line,' he spelt out coldly. 'You're my wife. It was our wedding day. No man would listen in silence when another man threw a challenge of that nature at him.'

'Joel did *not* challenge you!' Elvi proclaimed in heated disagreement.

An ebony brow skated up. 'It *wasn't* a challenge when Joel said he would be waiting to catch you *when* I messed up?'

Elvi stiffened and flushed. 'That was just one of those silly things a man says when he's trying to save face. You should've ignored it—'

'Consider me punching Joel as one of those silly things a man does when he's angry,' Xan advised lethally. 'Your compassion for him is misplaced—'

'No, it's not!' Elvi protested. 'I felt horribly guilty when he said he loved me because I felt that I should've noticed something. I wished I'd told him about you, for a start, but I didn't tell him about you because of the way our relationship started...*the arrangement*...we agreed.'

A faint line of colour scored Xan's killer cheekbones, the distaste with which she whispered those two explanatory words hitting him hard. 'Even when I wish I could, I *can't* change the past, Elvi,' he breathed in a driven undertone.

'No, but you can ensure you don't plough in and punch one of my friends again over something you overheard in a private conversation. Joel went too far but you went in fists flying and there was no need for it,' she told him stiffly.

'There was every need. Now he knows his boundaries but, since the violence upset you so much, I can assure you that it won't happen again,' Xan conceded grimly.

Only a little soothed, Elvi threw her head high. 'And you said I was *yours*,' she reminded him doggedly. 'I'm not. Putting a ring on my finger doesn't transform me into property.'

'You are mine,' Xan delivered in contradiction. 'Mine in a way no other woman has ever been.'

'Angie?' Elvi queried helplessly.

Xan compressed his lips. 'I didn't marry Angie or conceive a child with her.'

'But you didn't *intend* to do either of those things with me,' Elvi pointed out flatly.

Xan merely shrugged a dismissive big shoulder. 'Angie was my first love. We met at university. I fell hard for her,' he admitted harshly, his lean, strong face grim. 'I knew she was a material girl but it still didn't occur to me that if my prospects appeared to go downhill, she would choose money over me. There were rumours even before my father's death that his company was in trouble. Angie left me the same day the accountant confirmed that the family fortune was gone. She already had another man in her sights and within months she had married him and moved abroad.'

'You had a lucky escape,' Elvi told him staunchly. 'In the light of her behaviour why on earth did you make such a fuss of her at your sister's wedding?'

His spectacular bone structure pulled taut, amber-gold eyes shielded by his black lashes.

'I *had* to let you go. I was very much in the wrong dragging you into my bed in the first place and the only possible recompense I could make, after I discovered the extent of your innocence, was to let you return to your life,' he framed grittily. 'I *should* have let you go free that first day but I still wanted you too much. On Thira, wanting you, *needing* you to that extent freaked me out. Flirting with Angie gave me an escape route and forced me to set you free and I didn't have to tell you any lies—'

Elvi was stunned, listening in shaken silence to that unexpected confession because she had not appreciated how deep Xan's guilt over making her his mistress went. 'You make everything so complicated. You were behaving like one of those men who deliberately treats a woman badly to ensure that she breaks things off and saves him the trouble of doing it,' she mumbled in bemusement.

To be fair to her, her brain was working on more than one thought train. She was still thinking about Xan's surprising admission that needing her to such an extent had seriously worried him, which suggested to her that Xan had been feeling something more than lust for her, something strong enough to ignite his fear of a deeper commitment.

'But I've got you now,' Xan pointed out with unashamed satisfaction as he closed a powerful hand over hers and tugged her up out of her seat. 'I won't be treating you badly because I definitely don't want you to leave me—'

'You're sure of that?' Elvi checked. 'No more Angies or major affairs lurking in your past?'

'Not one. She burned me too badly. I protected myself after that,' Xan confessed huskily, his attention locking to Elvi's ripe pink mouth with smouldering intensity. That fast, he was aroused and aching for her.

He leant down to taste her in an exploratory foray that was supposed to be teasing, but which swiftly turned into a breathtakingly sensual assault. He plucked at the inviting fullness of her lower lip, traced the sealed line of her mouth with the teasing tip of his tongue and then plunged deep between her lips with the kind of hunger that made her tremble in his arms. A nagging hollow sensation deep down inside forced her to clamp her thighs tightly together.

'Were you jealous of Joel?' Elvi asked hopefully.

Xan drew back from her frowning. 'Of course not. I've never been the jealous type and since you won't be *seeing* him again—'

It was Elvi's turn to freeze. 'I beg your pardon?' she interrupted.

Xan shrugged. 'You can't see him again until he's got over you. If you keep on seeing him, you'll be encouraging him to continue wanting what he can't have. That would be cruel—'

'I can see him if I want to.'

'Not if I have anything to do with it,' Xan sliced in squarely. 'And why would you *want* to see him? He doesn't want to be your friend, he wants to be your lover.'

Elvi reddened uncomfortably, unable to escape the maddening reality that Xan was making valid points.

'He'll get over it eventually,' Xan forecast carelessly. 'If he had *really* loved you, he would have taken the risk and told you how he felt about you. But if you want my opinion—'

'I don't,' Elvi told him cuttingly.

'He knew if he told you how he felt about you he'd be plunging himself into a serious relationship and he wasn't ready for that. He kept you on ice for the future, encouraged by the fact that you weren't putting yourself out there for other men. He missed his chance.'

'You walked away from me too,' Elvi reminded him tightly.

'No, I *made* you walk away from me and it cost me. I've gone through a month of hell without you,' Xan murmured hoarsely, startling her with that grated confession. 'I haven't even looked at another woman since the day you came into my office—'

Elvi shook free of her disconcertion and treated him to an unimpressed appraisal. *'Angie?'*

'I was faking it,' Xan said drily.

Elvi settled down into her seat. 'You fake it

well,' she responded, stamping on the nugget of hurt that even thinking about that day recreated.

'I wanted you to believe I'd moved on.'

Purely because he had a guilty conscience about her? Or had he had other more personal reasons? Elvi speculated, not quite convinced that conscience could have driven Xan into creating a false picture when the more obvious solution would've been to let her go immediately. Had a desire for more sex been his sole motivator? There was so much she wanted to ask but Xan had that distant look back in his eyes again, suggesting that he had already given up enough in explanations for one day.

An SUV whisked them from the airport to the villa in the South of France. It was rural, which surprised her, a picturesque stone property surrounded by rolling lavender fields. A housekeeper greeted them. Xan went off for a shower while Elvi wandered round the cool interior, impressed by the clever mix of contemporary and antique that came together to create a relaxed atmosphere.

'Why did you buy this place if you hardly ever use it?' she asked him as he was getting dressed in lightweight chinos and a cotton shirt.

'I thought it would do me good to take holidays, but every time I came here I ended up working, so eventually I stopped coming,' he admitted wryly.

'I won't let you work while I'm here,' Elvi told him playfully.

Xan rested vibrant amber-gold eyes on her animated face. 'I don't want to work when you're around. You're bad for me.'

Elvi smiled at that very serious admission and, drawn by the glow of that encouraging teasing smile, he stalked across the room and grabbed her up into his arms, settling down again on the side of the bed with her cradled across his hard, muscular thighs.

'Sorry, I shouldn't have grabbed you like that, not when you're pregnant,' Xan breathed tautly. 'I need to be more careful—'

'The doctor told you I was perfectly healthy and strong,' Elvi reminded him.

Very deliberately, Xan splayed long brown fingers across her lower stomach. 'As far as I'm concerned, you're glass and breakable now,' he contradicted, smoothing her flesh gently. 'That's our child in there and we won't be taking any unnecessary risks.'

Warmth stole into Elvi, his concern banishing her fears. 'You really want this baby,' she murmured.

'As much as I want you, *moli mou*.' Xan lifted her up again and set her down on her feet with careful hands. 'Even if it was an unexpected development, it feels right now. Let's go downstairs and get dinner.'

Elvi gazed up into brilliant amber eyes and her heart skipped a beat. His fingers engulfed hers as he tugged her towards the stairs. He wanted their baby and he wanted her. It was sufficient to power a healthy start for any marriage, she told herself soothingly. Shame pierced her when she recalled *why* she had agreed to marry him, because she suspected she had fretted herself into an unreasonable state of paranoia when she worried that Xan might try to take her child from her.

Dinner was served out on the candlelit terrace. It was a light meal because neither of them was especially hungry. Over coffee, Xan studied her with hooded dark eyes, his lean bronzed face sombre. 'Why did you suddenly change your mind and decide to marry me?' he asked, sharply disconcerting her. 'I mean, you were saying no and so set against the idea and me and then, all of a sudden, you—'

It was now or never, Elvi registered, and, although she quailed at the prospect of telling him the unlovely truth, she also felt that she had to be honest. 'I was in a panic that day. I'd just found out I was pregnant,' she reminded him carefully in her own defence. 'I was very conscious that your father took you from your mother and I was scared that if we didn't get married, you might try to take our child from me at some time in the future.'

Xan frowned, staring at her in patent disbelief. 'I told myself that wives have more rights than unmarried mums and that your mother may not have fought for you but I would fight to hold on to any child of mine. I thought I'd be safer as a wife from that threat.' Her voice ran out of steam, her apprehension rising at the look of angry disbelief growing on his lean dark features.

'You can't be serious…' Xan intoned in a driven undertone.

'I'm not thinking that way any longer,' Elvi admitted ruefully. 'But unfortunately that *is* how I was thinking that day when I agreed—'

'I can't believe this,' Xan grated with a shake of his handsome dark head as he rose upright to stare across the table at her. 'I can't believe you actually thought that I would *do* that to you and my child after what I went through myself as a boy.'

'Yes, you did say you never felt secure—'

'It was a lot worse than that!' Xan objected, swinging away from her, suddenly short of breath and desperate to be alone. 'I'm going out for a drive—'

Elvi leapt out of her seat. 'Not without me, you're not!' she exclaimed.

'I'm not in the mood for company right now, Elvi,' Xan admitted harshly as he belatedly recognised that the mess of emotions he was experiencing all boiled down to that awful, ego-zapping word *hurt*, and the shock of that recognition hit him even harder.

What had he thought? That somewhere deep down inside Elvi had come to care for him? *Care* for the male who had virtually black-mailed her into his bed, into her first experience of sex and landed her into unplanned mother-hood at the same time? Naturally, caring had had nothing to do with her decision to marry him. Knowing nothing good of him, she had decided to protect herself in advance from any further wrong he might choose to inflict on her. How could he blame her for that?

Elvi planted herself in his path to the front door. 'No, Xan, you shouldn't be driving any-where when you're upset—'

Stormy amber-gold eyes locked to her. 'I'm *not* upset! Now move away from the door.'

'No.' Elvi stood her ground and when he tried to lift her to shift her to one side she swarmed up his lean, powerful body like a monkey climbing a tree and clung, her arms wrapping round his neck. 'Please talk to me, *please* don't walk away…don't hide things—'

His strong jawline setting hard like granite, Xan wrapped his arms round her to secure her and he carried her upstairs, where he lowered her down onto the bed. Or at least he *tried* to lower her, but Elvi was clinging like a limpet and when he tried to loosen her grip, she dropped her head and kissed him instead.

'No, Elvi,' he began doggedly.

Elvi threw her weight against him to unbalance him and he backed down on the bed to ensure that he didn't lose his balance. 'You don't mean no,' she told him with all the conviction of a woman who had come into contact with the noticeable bulge in his trousers. 'I won't let you leave me when you're upset.'

Xan groaned out loud and momentarily closed his eyes, trying to deny everything he was feeling. Meanwhile, Elvi hugged him tight and peppered his face with soothing kisses.

'*Thee mou*...what are you trying to do to me?' Xan ground out, engulfed by warm clingy woman and finding it surprisingly pleasant.

'Make you talk. I've explained myself as best as I can. I *had* to be honest. I won't lie to you,' Elvi stated. 'I was all over the place emotionally the day you asked me to marry you. I was still getting over the pain of you flirting with Angie and I didn't feel I could trust you at all. I was scared, confused and then I thought about how your father had taken you away from your mother and it petrified me.'

'I would never *do* that to you,' Xan intoned grimly. 'I had a hellish childhood living with my father.'

'Yes, I gathered that, but only recently. Initially you made your childhood sound idyllic.'

Xan groaned again, lush black lashes lifting on sombre amber-gold eyes. 'I always lie about it for my mother's sake. I don't like to hurt her. I don't want to make her feel guilty for not fighting for me because she really didn't have much choice,' he said grimly. 'My father replaced her with another woman and then insisted on keeping me as well. My grandparents persuaded Mum to go back to university to finish her Masters in the USA. She needed to get away from the island and she needed a new future to focus on. I have never blamed her for cutting her losses and running. She was still only a girl—'

Still perched on top of his big powerful body, Elvi ran gentle fingertips across the tightness of his wide sensual mouth as she bent over him. 'So, Ariadne went to America—?'

'And wrote and sold her first archaeology textbook. It was a bestseller—'

'While you were doing what?' she queried.

'Getting used to my first stepmother, Hana and Lukas's mother. That broke up when I was six and Dad moved another woman in. She didn't last but she gave birth to Tobias before she left. Wife number three came next and so it went on throughout my childhood and adolescence. Helios couldn't be faithful for five minutes and on a couple of occasions, between women, he even drifted back to Mum, causing her great distress,' he confided bitterly. 'He was a liar and a cheat and he pretty much ruined her life. She focused on her career and I saw very little of her until I reached my teens.'

'That must've been very difficult for you and your mother.'

'I'm very fond of her. She has a huge heart. She coped with losing me by burying herself in her studies and travelling round the world to work on archaeological digs—'

'What was it like for you growing up in such an unsettled household?' Elvi pressed, helplessly curious.

'Imagine what it's like to come home from school and discover your bedroom has been taken off you and given to a new step-sibling instead,' Xan urged. 'Nothing was permanent, nothing was private, nothing in the house on

Thira truly belonged to me. I was at the mercy of Dad's latest wife or lover. It made me a loner, who didn't trust anyone. I always thought my father married my mother too young and that's why he made such a mess but now I think he was just an easily bored womaniser.'

Elvi was drinking in every word, finally understanding how the boy had grown into a man with a colour-coded wardrobe and a powerful need for privacy. Deprived of order, control and security as a child, Xan had made order, control and security his first goals as an adult.

'Being a womaniser entails messy, dramatic relationships so I went the mistress route instead,' Xan confided. 'I suppose it was sleazy—'

'It *was* sleazy,' Elvi told him.

Xan shrugged a shoulder. 'It worked for me until you burst onto my horizon and then I blew it… I didn't want you in the same apartment where I'd been with other women. I didn't want to treat you the same way…'

As the silence dragged unbroken, Elvi stroked his lips apart with a tender fingertip and bent down to kiss him. 'If you talk, you get rewarded…and the more you talk, the bigger the reward gets,' she whispered encouragingly.

Xan arched his hips up beneath her, letting her know that his erection had not subsided. 'Tell me more, *moli mou*—'

'No, you bring out a side of me I don't know,' Elvi mumbled, suddenly embarrassed by her forward behaviour.

'You do the same to me. Unnerving, isn't it?' Xan prompted. 'I want you more than I've ever wanted a woman in my life—'

'Angie?' Elvi challenged shamefacedly.

'Angie was never a challenge. You were… Will you quit bringing her up?' he demanded impatiently.

Elvi nodded seriously. 'OK.'

'I thought you and I were just about good sex until I tried to make myself give you up. I felt huge guilt about depriving you of your virginity, but I still couldn't bring myself to let you go or admit that what I had with you was different from anything I'd ever had with a woman,' Xan told her, reaching up to untie the narrow shoulder straps of her sundress and tug her bodice down inch by dangerous inch.

'Stop it…we're talking!' Elvi protested.

'Can't we play at the same time?' Xan questioned, giving the dress a rough yank to free her full breasts, and then groaning out loud as her bountiful pale curves filled his hands to overflowing. 'I mean…let's be honest…at this moment… I will tell you *anything* you want to know—'

Her breath caught in her throat as he rubbed her swollen nipples between finger and thumb, sending a flash of heat shooting through her. 'Why were you trying to run away earlier?' she demanded shakily.

'I was…' Xan flung his tousled dark head back and breathed in deep and slow. 'When you told me you'd only married me because you were scared I might try to take our child away from you, I was…' Again he hesitated.

'You were…*what*?' Elvi prompted in frustration.

'Hurt… OK? I was *hurt*!' Xan finally got that word out and grimaced. 'Because by the time I got to our wedding today I knew I wanted and needed you round the clock and that somehow you had made me fall passionately in love with you, which explains why I continue to screw everything up. Passion and logic don't work well together and the way *you* make me feel often leaves me feeling like I'm clinging to sanity by my fingernails alone.'

Elvi gazed down at him in awed incredulity. 'You love me…*seriously*?'

'Serious as a heart attack.' Xan flipped over, carrying her with him, reversing their positions at the same time as he endeavoured to remove her dress. 'I think I started falling for you the minute I saw you, which is why I was so eaten up with guilt when I first took you to bed. Suddenly I was seeing every wrong thing I'd done and said to you in horrible Technicolor and I didn't know how to sort it out and start again.'

'You were hurt when you believed I'd married you just to safeguard my position.' Elvi smoothed gentle fingertips along his strong jaw while with her other hand she ran down the side zip on her dress to facilitate his manoeuvres. 'And I told myself I was agreeing for that reason, but I suspect that I was really giving myself a good reason to do what I secretly wanted to do because I love you. Do you deserve my love?' she asked for herself. 'No, you probably don't, but you can work at deserving it for the rest of our lives—'

Xan laughed out loud. 'I like it when you're blunt like that—'

'And, no, you don't get any time off for good behaviour,' she told him sternly. 'And after sex, you will always, *always* hold me close.'

'It's not just sex with you…it's much more than that,' Xan muttered awkwardly.

Elvi fluttered her eyelashes. 'Souls meeting?'

Xan laughed again, reaching down to kiss her at the same time as he unzipped his chinos. 'Our bodies are definitely going to meet,' he intoned against her reddened mouth with unconcealed hunger. 'On a collision course right now to that meeting—'

Being both a little frantic to make love again, they never did make it back downstairs for the dessert course and they lay talking lazily in bed until almost dawn. By that stage, they were involved in negotiations with Xan agreeing to take weekends and holidays off and Elvi agreeing not to drop clothes on the floor.

'I love you so much, *agape mou*,' Xan murmured, experiencing contentment for the first time ever, his beautiful eyes locked tenderly to Elvi's smiling, happy face. 'I'll buy you a dog once we've got used to being parents.'

Blissfully relaxed, Elvi let her arms tighten round his long, lean body, gentle fingers smoothing over his satin-smooth back. Xan liked to plan everything, cautiously moving from one checkpoint to the next. Yet without any preparation at all, he had plunged into their marriage and the promise of fatherhood with his whole heart, freely accepting those changes and loving her into the bargain.

'I love you too,' she whispered, happily convinced she had found a very special man.

Five years later, Elvi sat on the sand of the cove below the house on Thira and watched her daughter, Molly, patiently build a sandcastle with all the devotion to detail that Xan had already taught her. The little plastic flag had to go in exactly the right place, the moat had to fill with water, the shells that denoted windows had to sit in exact lines, and then disaster came along on two sturdy toddler legs. With a shout of delight, Molly's little brother, Ajax, flung himself at the castle, for he delighted as much in smashing things down as his sister delighted in building them.

But the split second before Ajax made contact and destroyed his sister's creation, a pair of arms stretched out and grabbed him back. 'No,' Xan told his son firmly.

Ajax wailed and screeched and struggled to escape his father's hold while Molly plonked herself defensively in front of the castle and told her brother off.

'When did you get back?' Elvi asked her husband, battling to be heard over Ajax's enraged yells.

'Ten minutes ago. The Athens meeting didn't last as long as I expected,' Xan told her with a lazy smile, quite unbothered by his son's vociferous complaints.

'Oh, let him wreck it,' Molly groaned in exasperation as her brother's sobbing reached an ear-splitting peak. 'The sea will take it tonight anyway.'

'Are you sure?' Elvi asked her daughter.

'He's a baby,' her daughter pointed out pityingly, anchoring herself to her father's side. 'I'll make another one tomorrow.'

Xan lowered Ajax back to the sand. The toddler hovered, tears sprinkling his chubby cheeks, his platinum-pale curls blowing in the breeze. He stretched out a chubby fist to bat at a tower and then overbalanced and fell on top of the castle, getting sand on his face, which he hated.

'It's really not his day,' Elvi pronounced as she rescued the little boy and brushed him free of sand while he watched her with the huge amber-gold eyes he had inherited from his father.

Their children were an endearing mix of their parents. Molly had black hair and blue eyes and a love of order. Ajax was two and he loved to make a mess. He was usually much quieter than Molly, except when he got overtired.

'He's ready for bed,' Elvi pronounced, gathering up the clutter around her and stuffing it into bags while Xan hoisted his son onto his shoulder. Holding Molly's hand, Xan led the way up the steep steps back to the house.

They'd had two children in five years and life was busy. Elvi had had an easy pregnancy with Molly and terrible morning sickness while carrying Ajax. She reckoned that their family was now complete. Their dog, a terrier mix called Bones, romped along in their wake, his frantic energy keeping his wiry little body fit in spite of a calorie intake that would have powered an elephant.

Their nanny whisked the children away for supper and bedtime and, having spent the entire day with her son and daughter, Elvi was grateful to have time for Xan. Xan might have given up his seven-days-a-week schedule but he was still very much in demand, flying round the world to make speeches and give advice. In the early days of their marriage she had travelled with him, but Molly's birth had intervened and their home base was now a very comfortable town house in London, convenient for Xan's office in the City. They spent holidays on Thira, finding the more laid-back lifestyle there perfect for raising their young family. When they wanted alone time as a couple, they flew to the South of France and left the grandparents in charge of their household.

Ariadne was an adoring grandmother but not as regularly available as Dmitri and Sally, who had, after a lengthy and very discreet relationship, married the year before at around the same time as Dmitri had taken early retirement. They now owned a house on the island and were regular visitors, just as Xan's siblings were. Family parties were regular events on Thira, and Elvi had become accustomed to hosting everything from barbecues to christenings. She loved the fact that their children were growing up with their cousins and enjoyed a wide circle of relatives, unlike herself.

Daniel had graduated in medicine and was now entering hospital training where his working hours would be very much longer. Elvi was grateful that her brother was based at a London hospital where she hoped to see more of him.

'You do appreciate that I have been away from you for an entire week,' Xan murmured, cornering her on the landing to extract a very hungry kiss from her willingly parted lips.

Her heart singing, Elvi gave him a sparkling smile.

'I *did* have this fantasy where you were waiting on the front step to greet me,' Xan told her as he walked her down to their bedroom.

'Like a Victorian servant?' Elvi asked with intense amusement dancing in her eyes.

'And then I had to go find you on the beach and you're covered in sand and windblown and…absolutely *gorgeous*,' Xan emphasised huskily, backing her down on the bed. 'And now you're going to get sand all over the bed—'

'Of course, if you're that fastidious I could go and have a shower first,' Elvi proffered, knowing he wouldn't have the patience to wait even three minutes.

Xan was undressing where he stood and nothing got hung up or carefully draped. Indeed, his tie, shoes and socks went flying. Of course, she knew he would tidy it all up afterwards and complain about the unfortunate effect she had on him. Confident that she was entirely the centre of his attention, Elvi shimmied seductively out of her sundress, skimmed off the last garments with panache and knelt on the bed, veiled in the hair he wouldn't let her cut. And as he studied her, she studied him, her breath catching in her throat as the long, taut muscular lines of his beautiful body emerged.

The hunger never died, she thought dreamily, turning her face up for his kiss, rejoicing in the fact that the whole world stopped for her when Xan was with her. It was the kind of happiness she had never hoped to find and *he* had given it to her, *he* had made her feel secure and adored and more precious than the diamonds he was continually gifting her.

'I love you,' she said softly. 'You never know your luck—I might wait on the front step for you the next time—'

'No, I like this…just you and me, *hara mou*,' Xan insisted, gathering her into his arms with a deep sigh of satisfaction, because coming home to his family, slipping back into the warm and happy atmosphere Elvi created for them, was the greatest pleasure of his life. 'Loving each other and living happily ever after… I didn't think I'd ever have that, but you gave it to me.'

* * * * *

LET'S TALK
Romance

For exclusive extracts, competitions and special offers, find us online:

f facebook.com/millsandboon

⬜ @millsandboonuk

🐦 @millsandboon

Or get in touch on 0844 844 1351*

For all the latest titles coming soon, visit millsandboon.co.uk/nextmonth

*Calls cost 7p per minute plus your phone company's price per minute access charge